THE
SHIPPING
NEWS

THE
SHIPPING
NEWS

Screenplay by
Robert Nelson Jacobs
based on the novel by
E. Annie Proulx

talk miramax books

HYPERION

NEW YORK

*This screenplay is dedicated
to the memory of my mother,
Merle Jacobs*

THE
SHIPPING
NEWS

EXT. AT THE EDGE OF A POND—DAY

We see IMAGES *of* YOUNG QUOYLE *(age 8) in a bathing suit, approaching the water, a half-step behind his burly* FATHER:

—Young Quoyle's SHUFFLING, WEAK-KNEED LEGS

—Young Quoyle's PALE HAND NERVOUSLY CLUTCHING A TOWEL

—Young Quoyle's DIM, NERVOUS EYES *glancing back and forth between the pond and the father who towers over him.*

—Young Quoyle's TOWEL DROPPING *from his slightly trembling hands, as he and his Father reach the pond's edge.*

TIGHT ON YOUNG QUOYLE, *who just stands there at the edge of the pond, paralyzed with anxiety.*

> QUOYLE'S FATHER
> *(gruff)*

Go on.

But Young Quoyle fearfully stays put.

> QUOYLE'S FATHER *(cont'd)*
Ain't got all day, boy.

Finally, Quoyle's Father disgustedly PUSHES THE BOY INTO THE WATER. *Young Quoyle frantically reaches up and grabs for his Father's leg—*

—and Quoyle's Father, with his heavy workboot, roughly shoves Quoyle away from shore.

QUOYLE'S FATHER *(cont'd)*
Christ. Move your arms. Kick your legs.

Quoyle's arms flail helplessly, water gurgling in his throat.

Quoyle's Father stolidly watches his son's horrible struggle.

YOUNG QUOYLE *sinks like a stone, air bubbling from his mouth and nose.*

YOUNG QUOYLE'S P.O.V.

Through the water we see the receding image of Quoyle's Father looking down with contempt, watching his son sink.

BACK ON YOUNG QUOYLE

sinking, sinking. We begin to hear MUFFLED, ECHOING VOICES OF KIDS AT PLAY.

YOUNG QUOYLE'S P.O.V.

Looking up to the water's surface, we see the phantom image of KIDS IN A PLAYGROUND *happily playing—and* YOUNG QUOYLE *(dressed for school) off in a corner away from the other kids, solitary, poking the ground with a stick.*

BACK ON YOUNG QUOYLE—WHO NOW MORPHS INTO 12-YEAR-OLD QUOYLE

Still sinking underwater. The sound of the kids at play now changes to the RAUCOUS, TAUNTING VOICES OF TEENAGE BOYS . . .

PHANTOM IMAGES SURROUND 12-YEAR-OLD QUOYLE, STILL UNDERWATER:

BOYS *in a locker room playing a malicious game of catch with Quoyle's underpants—while 12-Year-Old Quoyle ineffectually tries to intercept the underpants and laughs meekly, trying to pretend he's not humiliated.*

12-YEAR-OLD QUOYLE MORPHS INTO 16-YEAR-OLD QUOYLE

still sinking underwater, as the voices of the teenage boys change to the MUFFLED, ECHOING VOICES *of a* MAN AND WOMAN ARGUING . . .

QUOYLE'S P.O.V.

Looking through the water, he sees HIS FATHER VICIOUSLY SLAP HIS MOTHER—*and the Mother falls,* WEEPING, *and the Father stands over her,* YELLING *down at her, and:*

BACK ON 16-YEAR-OLD QUOYLE

sinking in the water, reaching out his arms as if to help his Mother—but of course he is powerless, sinking inexorably, and now he MORPHS INTO ADULT QUOYLE, *still sinking in the water, bubbles streaming from his mouth and nose . . .*

INT. MOVIE THEATER TICKET BOOTH—NIGHT

ADULT QUOYLE *stands in the old-fashioned, stand-alone ticket booth, dispensing tickets to* CUSTOMERS. *His gaze is bored and lifeless. The booth's glass is streaked with rain, making the faces of the Customers look distorted. Their* VOICES *are* MUFFLED . . . *We feel as though we're still underwater . . .*

INTERCUT:

QUOYLE UNDERWATER, *still sinking . . . sinking . . .*

INT. RESTAURANT KITCHEN—DAY

QUOYLE, *employed as a dishwasher, grabbing filthy dishes off a conveyor belt. The air is filled with* SPRAY AND STEAM, *making us feel like we're still underwater. The only sound is the echoing din and clank of dishes and silverware . . . Quoyle still has that bored, lifeless gaze . . .*

INTERCUT:

QUOYLE UNDERWATER, *endlessly sinking . . .*

INT. SMALL-TOWN NEWSPAPER—DAY

ADULT QUOYLE *has fallen asleep on the job: he's supposed to be pulling freshly printed newspapers off a conveyor belt. A* MAN *(Quoyle's* BOSS*) is shaking him awake:*

> BOSS
> Quoyle.

Quoyle stirs awake, looks up blearily at the BOSS. *We hear the* REPETITIVE, LETHARGIC, MUFFLED GROAN OF THE PRINTING PRESS.

> BOSS *(cont'd)*
> The job not stimulating enough for you?

> QUOYLE
> No. I mean yes. I mean—
> > *(sincerely; a plea:)*
> It's the best work I've ever had.

The Boss studies Quoyle a moment: is this guy serious?

> BOSS
> You must've had some fabulous jobs.

INTERCUT:

QUOYLE *sinking underwater . . .*

QUOYLE'S P.O.V.

Looking through a rain-streaked car windshield—and suddenly WINDSHIELD WIPERS DRAMATICALLY SWEEP THE WINDSHIELD CLEAN, *and we suddenly* LOSE THE FEELING OF BEING UNDERWATER, *and through the windshield we* SEE *with brilliant clarity:*
PETAL, *a fierce young woman of high sexual voltage,* SHRILLY QUARRELING *with a* MUSCULAR MAN. *Standing near a pump at a* GAS STATION, *Petal is wearing a slinky night-clubbing outfit.*

Quoyle, with slack-jawed wonder, is watching Petal's taunting, provocative way of quarreling.

Petal storms away from the Muscular Man. But the Muscular Man hurriedly follows her—grabs and kisses her. She hungrily kisses back for a moment—then abruptly pulls away and, without missing a beat, resumes FIERCELY QUARRELING. *Quoyle sits watching, fascinated.*

Petal notices Quoyle staring at her with abject awe. She likes that in a man.

Petal shoves the Muscular Man away from her, then hurries over to Quoyle's car, yanks open the door and leaps in.

PETAL
(to Quoyle)

Let's go.

Quoyle, stunned, paralyzed, just stares at her. The Muscular Man, glowering angrily, is heading toward the car.

Petal SLAPS QUOYLE'S FACE:

>   PETAL *(cont'd)*
> Wake up! Go!

A split-second before the Muscular Man reaches the car, Quoyle hits the gas, and off he goes with Petal.

>   QUOYLE
> Go where?

Petal smiles at Quoyle, her lips pearl-tinted and gleaming.

>   PETAL
> What's your name?

>   QUOYLE
> Quoyle.

>   PETAL
> I'm starving, Quoyle, aren't you?

INT. RESTAURANT—DAY

QUOYLE *watches in silent fascination as* PETAL *wolfs down steak and eggs.*

>   PETAL
> God, this hits the spot.
>   *(with her mouth full)*
> I sell burglar alarms.

Quoyle nods blankly.

>   PETAL *(cont'd)*
> You haven't touched your food.

He's been too busy gazing at her. Now he stupidly glances down at his plate.

>   QUOYLE
> Oh.

She smiles, enjoying his helpless attraction to her.

> PETAL
> What do you think? You want to marry me, don't you?

> QUOYLE
> *(soft, hoarse; meaning it:)*
> Yes.

Petal laughs. She curls her sharp-nailed fingers into his.

> PETAL
> *(a whisper)*
> It's 8:05. I think I'm going to fuck you by ten, what do you think of that?

INTERCUT:

QUOYLE *sinking in the water, his eyes wide and stupid . . .*

INT. QUOYLE'S APARTMENT BEDROOM—NIGHT

It's DARK, so all we can see is that PETAL, *semi-clothed, is on top. And we hear her* FIERCE, ECSTATIC SCREAMS.

CLOSE UP—QUOYLE'S FACE

Open-mouthed, wordless, gazing up at her with with awestruck gratitude. Drops of her sweat dripping down onto his face, like sweet gifts from above.

INT. THE BEDROOM—LATER

QUOYLE *and* PETAL *lie in each other's arms in a state of postcoital collapse. Petal heaves a satisfied sigh.*

> PETAL
> My God, that was the biggest one yet.

Now Petal reaches down to the floor and grabs her large purse. She opens it and begins pulling out food: chips, cookies, cheese.

> PETAL *(cont'd)*
> I'm always hungry after I get laid. I guess 'cause I burn up so many calories.

She begins eating the food without offering Quoyle any. Quoyle watches her. She looks around the room.

> PETAL *(cont'd)*
> You live in a dump, Quoyle.

> QUOYLE
> I love you.

Petal looks at Quoyle. After a moment, she holds out her chunk of cheese. Quoyle takes a little bite.

> PETAL
> *(in a little-girl voice)*
> Nibble, nibble, little mouse . . .

Quoyle chews on his cheese, gazing blissfully at Petal.

He is not speaking; we PRE-LAP *his* VOICEOVER:

> QUOYLE'S VOICE
> *(beseeching)*
> You're the only woman I've ever loved. Your name is written on my heart . . .

CUT TO:

INT. QUOYLE'S KITCHEN—DAY

ONE-YEAR-OLD BUNNY *is getting a bath in a plastic tub in the kitchen sink. Quoyle is bathing the infant while cradling a* PORTABLE PHONE *on his shoulder.*

QUOYLE *(continuing)*
(into phone)
. . . it's written on my heart forever. Petal. Petal.

Bunny is fussing in her tub. Quoyle tries to quiet her.

PETAL (V.O./PHONE)
(casual, indifferent)
How do you make an Alabama Slammer?

Through the phone, Quoyle can hear the background noise of a crowded honky-tonk.

QUOYLE
Petal, sweetheart . . . Where are you?

PETAL (V.O./PHONE)
Alabama. That's why I'm asking.

Quoyle swallows.

PETAL (V.O./PHONE) *(cont'd)*
Look up the recipe. On the fridge, where I keep the Mr.
Boston.

QUOYLE
(a wretched plea)
If you come home, I'll make one for you.

PETAL (V.O./PHONE)
Oh Christ, never mind.

CLICK. *She has hung up.*

INTERCUT:

QUOYLE *sinking in the water, sinking, sinking into the murk . . .*

INT. QUOYLE'S BEDROOM—NIGHT (YEARS LATER)

SIX-YEAR-OLD BUNNY *lies in asleep in Quoyle's bed, clutching a* BABY DOLL. QUOYLE *lies next to her, vacantly watching TV.*

A KEY JIGGLES *in the front door. Quoyle looks up, nervous and hopeful. He peers out into:*

INT. HALLWAY—SAME

And he's heartened to see PETAL *striding in, a little drunk, sexy as ever. Quoyle wants to call out to her—but his voice catches in his throat when he sees: a* YOUNG HUNK *stumbling in after Petal, drunkenly finding her ass with his hand.*

> PETAL
> *(to the Hunk)*
> You want to marry me, don't you?

INT. THE BEDROOM—A LITTLE LATER

QUOYLE, *in misery, lies in bed listening to the* SOUNDS OF VIOLENT, HYSTERICAL SEX *from the living room.*

INTERCUT:

QUOYLE *sinking in the water, down, down, until he* HITS ROCK BOTTOM.

FADE TO BLACK.

FADE IN:

INT. BATHROOM—MORNING

PETAL, *in a velvet bra, is squeezing into a pair of impossibly tight jeans.* QUOYLE *enters.*

QUOYLE
(deferential)
Is your friend gone?

PETAL
(smirks)
My "friend"?

Quoyle, with ineffable longing, watches Petal squeeze into the skin-tight jeans and throw on a flimsy blouse.

Quoyle, aroused by the sight of Petal getting dressed, cautiously approaches and leans toward her, hoping just to kiss her—but she fiercely spins away from him:

PETAL *(cont'd)*
Don't do that. Don't touch me!

QUOYLE
(backs away)
Sorry.

After a moment, Petal sees (in the mirror) Quoyle straightening up toiletries.

PETAL
Stop doing stuff! Creeping around, cleaning up.

She assesses him a moment. A word to the wise:

PETAL *(cont'd)*
Look, it's no good. Find yourself a girlfriend.

QUOYLE
I don't want . . . I only want you.

PETAL
(shrugs)
Your funeral.

Petal picks up an open can of beer:

> PETAL *(cont'd)*
> To your health.

She takes a swig and heads out.

INT. THE LIVING ROOM—A MOMENT LATER

Quoyle sadly watches Petal head for the door.

> QUOYLE
> Will you be home tonight? Bunny's been missing you. I could cook something—

> PETAL
> Don't expect me.

Now BUNNY sleepily wanders out from her room.

> BUNNY
> Hey Petal.

> PETAL
> Hey Bunny Rabbit. Petal's gotta run.

> BUNNY
> *(points to Petal's necklace:)*
> That's so pretty.

Petal yanks off the POP-TOP *from her beer can, kneels down and slips the pop-top's little loop onto the tip of Bunny's pinky.*

> PETAL
> *(breezy, without much feeling; re: pop-top on Bunny's pinky)*
> So's that.

Bunny regards her little pop-top ring with pride. Petal starts to get up . . . but Bunny impulsively reaches up to Petal's necklace—and the cheap necklace BREAKS, *its beads* CASCADING *onto the floor.*

PETAL *(cont'd)*
Shit.

Petal heads out, and the screen door slams behind her.

BUNNY
(to Quoyle; re: scattered beads)
Sorry.

INT. THE NEWSPAPER—DAY

QUOYLE *doing his boring, repetitive job pulling newspapers off the conveyor belt. He's got the glazed eyes of a dead man. The only sound is the* ENDLESS, MUFFLED CLANK AND GROAN *of the printing press.*

INT. NEWSPAPER LUNCHROOM—DAY

NEWSPAPER EMPLOYEES *sit at tables, eating talking, laughing; it's a lively place.*

But sitting at a small table in the corner is QUOYLE, *silent, alone, chomping on a big greasy cheeseburger.*

INT. OFFICES OF THE GAZETTE-JOURNAL—DAY

The NEWSPAPER EMPLOYEES *are returning to the city room after lunch.* QUOYLE *enters last, alone. He is still stuffing down an eclair as he heads back to work.*

There's one answering machine for everybody at the newspaper, glowing a red number 2.

Someone hits the answering machine button.

FEMALE VOICE (V.O./ANSWER MACHINE)
Danny, it's Lila. Ten-thirty. Bring the . . . you know.

Danny doesn't even bother to smirk. A shrug is plenty.

FATHER (V.O./ANSWER MACHINE)
(tired, brusque)
Quoyle, this is your father. Lost your home number. It's
time for your mother and I to go.

Quoyle listens, puzzled.

FATHER (V.O./ANSWER MACHINE) *(cont'd)*
I left instructions with the undertaker, Dayton & Sons. Told
'em to notify my sister, Agnis Hamm.

Quoyle is stunned. People are sneaking looks at him.

FATHER (V.O./ANSWER MACHINE) *(cont'd)*
Not much of a life. Nobody gave me nothin'. Other men
would of given up and turned into bums, but I didn't.

Everybody's staring at Quoyle now.

FATHER (V.O./ANSWER MACHINE) *(cont'd)*
I wheeled barrows of sand for the stonemason. I went
without so you could have advantages, not that you done
anything with them—

The answer machine BEEPS.

ELECTRONIC VOICE
That was your final message.

Quoyle is fighting tears.

A NEWSPAPER EMPLOYEE
Were they sick or something?

QUOYLE
Brain tumor and liver cancer.
(then, awkwardly:)
One apiece.

INT. A DIMLY LIT BAR—DAY

PETAL, *sitting at the bar, is talking on a portable* PHONE:

> PETAL
> Oh come on, they must've left *some*thing. What's their house worth?

> QUOYLE (V.O./PHONE)
> The bank's taking it. There's nothing.

Petal shakes her head in disgust.

> QUOYLE (V.O./PHONE) *(cont'd)*
> Petal? Sweetheart?

Petal casually hangs up the phone, hands it back to the BARTENDER, *a handsome guy in a* HAWAIIAN SHIRT. *He's eying her body. She flashes him a sexy smile.*

INT. QUOYLE'S HOUSE—BEDROOM

PETAL *stands on a chair, pulling one suitcase and then another off a high closet shelf.* BUNNY *is watching her.*

> BUNNY
> *(excited)*
> I won't have to go to school?

> PETAL
> It's an adventure. Who goes to school when they're on an adventure?

Bunny squeals with excitement. Petal hurriedly pulls clothes out of the closet and shoves them into the suitcases.

> BUNNY
> Is Daddy coming?

PETAL
(shakes her head no)
Daddy's boring.

INT./EXT. QUOYLE'S HOUSE—DAY

The baby-sitter, a surly young woman named GRACE, has taken her eyes off the TV screen to watch:

PETAL, big tote bag over her shoulder, suitcases in both hands, herding BUNNY (who carries a backpack) towards the front door.

PETAL
There's Dave. Come on, he's waiting.

They see the BARTENDER (the guy in the Hawaiian shirt) in his RED CONVERTIBLE outside the house.

EXT. QUOYLE'S HOUSE—SAME

PETAL leads BUNNY toward the Bartender's convertible.

GRACE
(from the house)
Hey—what about my pay? You owe me for three weeks!

CUT TO:

INT. LIVING ROOM—LATER

QUOYLE, wearing an ILL-FITTING BLACK SUIT, has just entered carrying TWO CREMATION URNS. He is confronting an impassive GRACE, who still sits in front of the TV.

QUOYLE
(upset)
Took Bunny? What do you mean, she "took" Bunny?

GRACE
(shrugs)
I think she mentioned Florida.

Quoyle is stunned, speechless.

> GRACE *(cont'd)*
> You owe me for three weeks a baby-sittin'.

CUT TO:

NIGHT—QUOYLE PACING AROUND THE LIVING ROOM

in a frenzy of anxiety. He stops to pick a speck of lint off the carpet, looks at his watch, resumes pacing fretfully.

There's a KNOCK *at the door. Quoyle races over, yanks it open—*

—but it's not Petal. It's AGNIS HAMM, *a stiff-figured old woman. Quoyle stares at her in consternation.*

> AGNIS
> *(flinty)*
> Agnis Hamm. Half-sister of Guy Quoyle. I'm your aunt.

> QUOYLE
> This is a bad time—

> AGNIS
> So I heard. I'm here to visit his ashes.

> QUOYLE
> No, I mean a really, really bad time.

Agnis stares, sizing him up. She sees the anguish in his eyes, realizes he's struggling to hold himself together.

CUT TO:

INT. QUOYLE'S LIVING ROOM—LATER

AGNIS *brings two cups of tea to the coffee table, where Quoyle sits miserably chomping on potato chips.*

QUOYLE

She's never done this. I mean, she's walked out before—but
never with Bunny. I just can't understand—

AGNIS

The potato chips won't do you any good. Drink the tea.

QUOYLE

Pardon?

AGNIS

Tea's a good drink. It'll keep you going.

Quoyle puts down the chips.

QUOYLE
(like a needy child)
Could you . . . maybe stay for a while?

AGNIS

Sorry, just passing through.

She motions for Quoyle to drink his tea. He does.

AGNIS *(cont'd)*
On my way up to Newfoundland, where our people are
from. You ever been there, nephew?

Quoyle shakes his head no.

AGNIS *(cont'd)*
Thought I'd never go back. But the older you get . . . There's
a pull. An ache. Something you got to figure out. Like
you're a piece in a puzzle.

Quoyle sips the tea.

AGNIS *(cont'd)*
Just wanted to say farewell to Guy first.
(let's get it over with:)
If you'll show me where he is.

                              QUOYLE
Oh. Yeah, sorry.

He looks over at TWO URNS *on a table.*

                              QUOYLE *(cont'd)*
He's on the left.

The PHONE RINGS. *Quoyle suddenly rushes out into the kitchen.*

INT. KITCHEN—SAME

Quoyle has urgently picked up the phone.

                              QUOYLE
Hello? Hello?

It's a bad connection, lots of static.

                              QUOYLE *(cont'd)*
Petal—is that you?

                    OFFICER DANZIG (V.O./PHONE)
Mr. Quoyle?

                              QUOYLE
                       (apprehensive, urgent)
Yes. Yes? Hello?

                    OFFICER DANZIG (V.O./PHONE)
Mr. Quoyle, this is Officer Danzig from the state police—

                              QUOYLE
                          (breathless)
Oh Jesus—did you find them?

INTERCUT BETWEEN QUOYLE TALKING ON THE PHONE AND THE FOLLOWING ACTION:

INT. LIVING ROOM—SAME

AGNIS, *alone in the living room, hurriedly pulls an oversized* ZIPLOC BAG *from her large carpetbag purse. She reaches toward her brother's urn. For a moment her hand quivers—it's emotional torture for her even to touch the urn—*

—but then, with steely resolve, she snatches the urn and removes its lid . . . and in one swift movement pours the ashes into the Ziploc bag.

From her purse she takes out ANOTHER ZIPLOC BAG FILLED WITH OTHER ASHES. *She pours the "decoy ashes" into the urn, quickly replaces the lid . . . and furtively shoves the Ziploc containing her brother's ashes into her purse.*

> OFFICER DANZIG (V.O./PHONE)
> We found your daughter, sir.

> QUOYLE
> Thank God. And Petal?

> OFFICER DANZIG (V.O./PHONE)
> Uh, Mr. Quoyle, we're enroute now. We'll talk when we get there.

In the living room, AGNIS *quickly closes her purse a split-second before* QUOYLE *reenters the room.*

> QUOYLE
> They're bringing Bunny. The police. She's okay.

> AGNIS
> Thank God. What about your wife?

Quoyle gives Agnis a worried, uncertain look.

EXT. A RIVERBANK—NIGHT

where POLICE *and* BYSTANDERS *are gathered. A* WINCH *is pulling something up from the river depths.*

PRE-LAP:

> OFFICER DANZIG (V.O.)
> The convertible went over a guardrail down in Jersey. They weren't even wearing seat belts, your wife and her, uh, male companion.

Part of the RED CONVERTIBLE *now comes up out of the river, streaming water and mud as the winch lifts it.* PETAL'S LIFELESS BODY *hangs over the side of the car, her arms outstretched like a ballet dancer.*

EXT. QUOYLE'S HOUSE—NIGHT

OFFICER DANZIG *(whose* SQUAD CAR *is parked at the curb) is speaking to* QUOYLE, *who is in a state of shock.* AGNIS *listens stoically.*

> OFFICER DANZIG
> She was mercifully killed on impact, I can promise you.

Quoyle just looks numbly at the Officer.

> OFFICER DANZIG *(cont'd)*
> And I'm afraid there's . . . something else.

Quoyle looks at the Officer in confusion: something else?

> OFFICER DANZIG *(cont'd)*
> Seems she sold your daughter to a black market adoption outfit for six thousand dollars.

Quoyle looks like he's going to faint.

> OFFICER DANZIG *(cont'd)*
> There's a receipt, if you can imagine. That's how we tracked her.

A SECOND SQUAD CAR *pulls up, and* OFFICER #2 *escorts* BUNNY *out of the car.*

Quoyle, his eyes glazed, goes to Bunny.

> QUOYLE
>
> Hi, sweetheart.

He gives her a candy bar, and opens one for himself. Unsmiling, Bunny takes a big bite out of her candy bar.

> BUNNY
> *(points to Agnis)*
>
> Who's that?

> AGNIS
>
> "That" is your Great Aunt Agnis.

> BUNNY
>
> Oh.
> *(annoyed, to Quoyle)*
> Where's Petal?

> QUOYLE
>
> She's . . .

Quoyle is choked up, can't speak. Bunny irritably brushes past him and runs into the house.

Quoyle just stands there, paralyzed with grief and confusion.

> AGNIS
> *(to Quoyle)*
> Maybe I could stay just a day or two.

EXT. QUOYLE'S TINY, WEED-CHOKED BACKYARD—DAY

QUOYLE *and* BUNNY *sit together on the back stoop. Quoyle is holding a* BOOK: A Child's Introduction to Departure of a Loved One.

QUOYLE
"Your loved one has not gone from your heart or from your thoughts, but is sleeping peacefully."

AGNIS *watches and listens through the screen door, clearly disapproving of the euphemistic language of self-help.*

BUNNY
Will she wake up?

QUOYLE
No, Bunny.

BUNNY
But she's sleeping?

QUOYLE
Peacefully. In heaven. With the angels.

Agnis shakes her head, and disappears into the house.

BUNNY
If I was asleep, I'd wake up.

Bunny studies Quoyle's face for a moment. Then:

BUNNY *(cont'd)*
Why are you so scared, Daddy?

Quoyle doesn't know what to say. He's struggling not to cry.

INT. THE KITCHEN—LATER

AGNIS *is cleaning up the messy place, stoically scrubbing breakfast bowls crusted with week-old cereal.*

BUNNY *enters and observes Agnis at work.*

BUNNY
What are you doing?

                         AGNIS
        It's called cleaning.

Agnis hands Bunny a dish and a dish towel.

                    AGNIS *(cont'd)*
        Here. Dry this.

Bunny looks at the dish and then back at Agnis.

                         BUNNY
        You're boring.

Agnis raises an eyebrow: what *did you say?*

But then they begin to hear o.s. SOBBING. *Agnis dries her hands
and walks out of the kitchen, with Bunny following.*

INT. BEDROOM—SAME

AGNIS *enters, and sees* QUOYLE *on the bed,* SOBBING *like a
child, his face buried in a pillow. He's clutching a* SILK
NIGHTGOWN, *holding it the way a child holds a security blanket.*

                         AGNIS
                   (quietly, to Quoyle)
        Stop that.

*But Quoyle keeps sobbing, clutching the nightgown. Agnis darkly
watches him. Then:*

                    AGNIS *(cont'd)*
        That's enough now.

Quoyle looks up at Agnis, like a questioning child.

EXT. FERRY—LONG SHOT—DAY

The ferry moves through dark choppy northern waters.

> AGNIS (V.O.)
> It takes a year, Nephew, a full turn of the calendar, to get over losing somebody.

EXT. DECK OF THE FERRY—DAY

AGNIS *sits on a bench facing the sea.*

> AGNIS
> That's a true saying. The move'll help. You'll see.

Now we find QUOYLE, *seasick, fighting nausea, weakly semi-reclining on the bench next to Agnis.*

> AGNIS *(cont'd)*
> What place on this earth could be more right than the place your people came from? You smell that clean northern sea?

She glances over at Quoyle—who is swallowing desperately, trying not to vomit.

> QUOYLE
> I'm not a water person.

> AGNIS
> Hm. Well, at least the girl is.

Agnis indicates BUNNY *over near the bow, eagerly pressed up against the rail, catching the mist of sea-spray on her face.*

> QUOYLE
> I hope we're doing the right thing, Aunt.

She gazes at the far-off land they're approaching.

AGNIS
(quietly)
Truth be told, I'm glad for the company.

Quoyle notices that Bunny is staring at something farther down the deck. Quoyle follows Bunny's gaze to see what she's looking at:

A honey-haired MOTHER *(WAVEY PROWSE), in a parka, woolen skirt, stockings and heavy boots, is holding her 4-year-old* BOY *(HERRY) in her lap, feeding him an apple with great tenderness. The Mother is talking to the Boy, calmly, carefully, as if imparting something of meaning and value . . . but the Boy's face is blissfully vacant.*

Quoyle watches. The Mother, as if suddenly aware she's being watched, casually glances up in Quoyle's direction—and Quoyle instantly looks away.

THE FERRY

is now in sight of an old-fashioned LIGHTHOUSE *on a rocky little islet.*

EXT. COAST—GREAT NORTHERN PENINSULA (AERIAL)—DAY

CAMERA SWEEPS IN *over the coast road, showing us the great fissured rock; cracked cliffs in volcanic glazes; tombstone houses jutting from raw granite. And on the horizon: icebergs.*

AGNIS (V.O.)
Nothing grows up here on the rock, nothing you can use. We left it fifty years ago, us Quoyles. Hard times. Oh, I remember the stories. Failed fishermen with heads like skulls.

CAMERA FINDS: QUOYLE'S STATION WAGON, *riding up the coast road.*

A scrawny old grandfather who shot himself so the family could get by—one less stomach to fill. Children surviving on flour scrapings and boiled pork bones.
(a BEAT)
We're almost there.

INT. QUOYLE'S STATION WAGON—DAY

QUOYLE *at the wheel;* AGNIS *holding a map;* BUNNY *in the backseat repeatedly buckling and unbuckling her seat belt, an idle game.*

AGNIS
(points to map)
Right here: Quoyle Point. Named after us. You.

As Quoyle gazes out at the beautiful but hostile landscape, he feels a mix of awe and anxiety.

QUOYLE
Lot of snow.

BUNNY
Is it already Christmas, Daddy?

QUOYLE
(troubled; eying snow)
No. It's May. Seven months to go.

AGNIS
Up here, forget everything you thought you knew about weather.
(notices Bunny buckling and unbuckling seat belt)
Stop that, child.

EXT. QUOYLE'S POINT—SUNSET

The station wagon pulls up in a shroud of mist. QUOYLE, AGNIS, *and* BUNNY *climb out. They stare into what seems like the center of a dense cloud, until . . .*

. . . *the* FOG LIFTS. *And like a ghost, a* GREEN HOUSE *appears. Then* DISAPPEARS *in the fog. Then* APPEARS *again.*

> AGNIS
> *(quietly)*
>
> I was born there.

> BUNNY
>
> Green. Yuck.

The house stands alone on a rocky point. Half the windows are gone; holes in the roof, paint flaking. A forbidding place.

> AGNIS
>
> Empty forty-four years, and look at that roofline. Straight as a ruler.

> BUNNY
>
> I don't like the green.

> AGNIS
> *(sharply)*
>
> So you said.

EXT. THE GREEN HOUSE—SUNSET

QUOYLE *and* BUNNY *watch* AGNIS *trying to force open the front door—which is warped and stuck. Agnis impatiently* KICKS *the door, forcing it to creak open. The three of them apprehensively enter.*

INT. LIVING ROOM OF GREEN HOUSE—SUNSET

AGNIS, QUOYLE, *and* BUNNY *look around this musty, corroded sanctum.*

QUOYLE *picks up a cracked photo from a pile of junk: it shows a* BOY, *8, with the look of a Quoyle, in a seal-fur coat.*

                         AGNIS
Your grandfather, Sian Quoyle.
He died before I was born. Sweet-natured fella, they say.
                    (with a slight twinkle in the eye)
It skips a generation.
                         (looks back at photo)
They say when he went under the ice he called out, "See
you in heaven." Died young—twelve years old.

                        QUOYLE
Twelve? Then he couldn't've been my grandfather.

                         AGNIS
You don't know Newfoundlanders.

                         BUNNY
                    (finding another photo)
Who's this?

It's a picture of a different QUOYLE BOY, *a stocky and sullen 15-
year-old, standing by a frozen pond; next to him, a husky raw-boned
GIRL of 12 in a woolen hat. There's a flatness in the Girl's gaze;
not showing any hint of feeling . . .*

*. . . which is much like the look in Agnis's eyes right now, as she
considers the photo.*

                        QUOYLE
                        (realizing:)
My father. And you?

                         AGNIS
                       (no emotion)
I never did care for that hat.

Agnis moves on, leading the way into:

INT. THE KITCHEN—SAME

> AGNIS
> *(can hardly believe she's back)*
> There's the stove, hasn't moved a centimeter—and oh my
> lord the table, the blessed table.

> QUOYLE
> There's no way we can live here.

> AGNIS
> It's all fixable.

Bunny opens a drawer to see if anything's inside—and the drawer, all rotted, crumbles to the floor.

Quoyle gives the aunt a dubious look.

> AGNIS *(cont'd)*
> We'll get a carpenter.

> QUOYLE
> Might be cheaper to build a new house—on the Riviera.

> AGNIS
> Only I wasn't born on the Riviera.

Bunny runs upstairs.

INT. UPSTAIRS IN THE GREEN HOUSE—TWILIGHT

BUNNY *walks down the hallway, eying the dilapidated rooms with wary curiosity.*

> AGNIS (O.S.)
> So let's see, some new windows, insulation and wallboard.
> Replace the roof, of course. Fix chimneys. Repair the
> waterline from the spring . . .

Bunny now sees AGNIS, with QUOYLE following, coming upstairs.

AGNIS *(cont'd)*
We can bring in the sleeping bags, camp here.

Agnis and Quoyle are walking over to Bunny.

AGNIS *(cont'd)*
It'll be an adventure, eh?

Quoyle, skeptical, looks down at his daughter—who nods, as if Agnis had made a perfectly natural suggestion.

BUNNY
Which one's Petal's room? I'll sleep there.

Agnis gives Quoyle a sharp look, as if prompting him to correct Bunny's delusion. But Quoyle only shrugs sheepishly.

EXT. THE GREEN HOUSE—NIGHT

A storm rages. The torrential rain is washing away the snow.

INT. A BEDROOM IN THE GREEN HOUSE—NIGHT

QUOYLE *is asleep in a sleeping bag. (*AGNIS *is asleep in a sleeping bag in the other bedroom across the hall.) But* BUNNY *is wide awake, standing by the window a few feet away from Quoyle . . . she's looking out at the* CABLES *that secure the house to the rocky earth. Outside, the rainfall is washing the snow away; and in the fierce wind, the* CABLES *make a* WEIRD, ALMOST-MUSICAL, MOANING SOUND, *like an eerie off-key string quartet.*

Bunny, fearful and agitated, goes over to Quoyle and starts flicking his ear with her finger until he wakes up.

QUOYLE
(groggy)
What . . . ?

He sees Bunny. He pats the empty sleeping bag next to him:

QUOYLE (cont'd)

Go to sleep, sweetie.

BUNNY

No. I don't want to.

QUOYLE

Why'd you wake me up?

Bunny shrugs. She returns to the window. Quoyle watches her a moment, then he closes his eyes again.

CAMERA PUSHES IN *on* QUOYLE'S FACE *as he drifts back to sleep . . . and we DISSOLVE TO:*

EXT. PHANTOM UNDERWATER SCENE

A murky, greenish underwater world. PETAL *is languidly swimming, her dress billowing about her thighs.*

Now reveal QUOYLE *in the water behind Petal, trying to pursue her—but he can't swim.*

Petal glances back at him, laughs soundlessly, and flirtatiously waves for him to come join her.

But Quoyle is drowning, bubbles streaming from his nose; his mouth open in a silent scream . . .

QUOYLE SUDDENLY WAKING UP FROM HIS DREAM

in his sleeping bag, in the Green House. He's upset by the dream. It is MORNING. *Bunny's sleeping bag is empty.*

EXT. THE GREEN HOUSE—MORNING

QUOYLE, *shivering, emerges from the house, his breath steaming. He sees* AGNIS *standing by a campfire, sleeping bag wrapped around her like a royal robe; she stirs a bubbling pot of* OATMEAL.

32

Quoyle sees Bunny scampering nearby, inspecting rocks, etc.

Agnis pours oatmeal into a tin camping cup, hands it to Quoyle.

He tastes it . . . and it warms him.

Bunny tugs on one of the cables that anchor the house . . .

> QUOYLE
> *(re: cables)*
> Are those to keep the house from blowing away?

> AGNIS
> So far so good.

This is not reassuring to Quoyle.

> AGNIS *(cont'd)*
> Before my time. They said it rocked in storms like a big
> rocking chair. Made the women sick, so they lashed it down.

> BUNNY
> The house is sad.

> QUOYLE
> What?

Bunny keeps tugging on a cable, as if trying to snap it.

> BUNNY
> You should let it loose.

Quoyle raises an eyebrow. Bunny scampers off.

EXT. THE GAMMY BIRD—DAY

*A two-bit local newspaper office. The sign out front features a
painted quacking duck.*

QUOYLE'S STATION WAGON *pulls up in front of this ramshackle little building.* QUOYLE, *wearing his* ILL-FITTING BLACK SUIT, *nervously gets out of the car. He vainly tries to readjust his off-kilter necktie. He goes to the door and takes a deep breath, trying to work up the nerve to go inside.*

An ANCIENT TOYOTA *pulls up to the building, and out flounces* TERT X. CARD, *a man who never smiles except in derision. Card hurries to the door—where Quoyle still stands indecisively with his hand on the doorknob.*

> CARD
> Are you going in, or you just going to fondle the doorknob?

> QUOYLE
> I'm here to apply for a job.

Card snorts incredulously. He motions for Quoyle to follow him into the office.

Quoyle blinks a few times, then goes inside after Card.

INT. THE GAMMY BIRD—SAME

The "newsroom," a cramped office of faded walls and cracked linoleum flooring, is currently manned by two Reporters. One is B. BEAUFIELD NUTBEEM, *a Brit with buttery hair swept behind his ears, plaid bowtie and a ratty pullover. Nutbeem is hunched over an old, staticky* SHORTWAVE RADIO. *The tuning knob is broken-off; Nutbeem uses a table knife to twist the slot, tuning the shortwave to an English-language broadcast about women being stoned to death in Third World countries.*

Card leads Quoyle past the other Reporter, BILLY PRETTY, *a wiry man in his 70s, his face engraved with wrinkles. His desk looks like a church bazaar: straw baskets, wooden butterflies, babies' booties in dime-store nylon, eggs decorated with watercolor faces.*

BILLY
(into phone; consulting written notes)
I need clarification on this. I've got Doris Koontz down as
Runner-Up in "Cakes and Muffins"—but her entry is listed
as Strawberry-Rhubarb Cobbler, which I believe oughta be
under "Pies."

As Card passes, he and Billy glower poisonously at each other.

Card leads Quoyle into a small, shabby PRIVATE OFFICE.

CARD
(cranky; loudly declaiming:)
I am Tert Card, the managing editor, rewrite man, and snow
shoveller. You'll have to do without the boss. Himself, Jack
Buggit, has called in sick as usual.

(SHOUTS to Billy, through half-open door:)
Which is why I am occupying his office, and no bones about
it!

Billy glares at Card; it's clear this is an ongoing argument.

CARD *(cont'd)*
Name?

QUOYLE
Me? Quoyle. I—

CARD
(looking him over)
A Quoyle, are you? Well. I should of seen that right off.

Quoyle shifts in his seat, uncomfortable under Card's critical stare.

QUOYLE
Is there an application I could—

                              CARD

Prior experience as a journalist. *Washington Post? London
Times?*

                             QUOYLE

Journalist . . . no no. Print line operator. I just wondered if
you might need—

The PHONE RINGS, *and Card snatches it up:*

                              CARD

Gammy Bird.

                      JACK (V.O./PHONE)
                       (with suspicion)
Are you in my office, Tert?

                              CARD
                      (caught off-guard)
What? No no. Just conducting a job interview here at my
desk—

                     JACK (V.O./ PHONE)
Job interview?

                              CARD

There's a Mr. Quoyle—

                  JACK'S VOICE (V.O./PHONE)
The fella's a Quoyle, you say? As in Q-U-O-Y-L-E?

                              CARD
                      (studying Quoyle)
And no mistake.

                  JACK'S VOICE (V.O./PHONE)
Hm.
                            (a BEAT)
Have him meet me at the dock in one hour.

CARD

That bronchitis of yours cleared up already?

INTERCUT WITH:

EXT. JACK'S FISHING BOAT—SAME

JACK BUGGIT, *a ruggedly handsome old salt—the very picture of health—is talking into his* MOBILE PHONE *while he fishes.*

JACK

Much better. 'Preciate your concern.

CUT TO:

EXT. KILLICK-CLAW DOCK—LATER

QUOYLE parks his station wagon, gets out and looks around.

JACK BUGGIT *is sitting in his docked boat (which has the words "Maid in the Meadow" painted on its stern),* GUTTING FISH *with a huge knife. He sees Quoyle.*

JACK

Quoyle—over here, step lively.

Quoyle approaches . . . but stops at the edge of the dock. Jack looks him over.

QUOYLE

Mr. Buggit—

JACK

The name is Jack.

Quoyle looks at the boat swaying ever-so-gently in the water.

JACK *(cont'd)*

Well come on, get in.

37

QUOYLE

I'm not a water person.

JACK

All Quoyles is water people. Boats is in your blood.

Quoyle works up his courage, and steps gingerly into the gently rocking boat. He sits down and nervously clutches the sides of the vessel. Jack eyes him a moment.

JACK *(cont'd)*

That's why I'm hiring you. I need somebody to cover the shipping news. You'll get the list from the harbormaster—what ships come into Killick-Claw, what ones goes out.

QUOYLE
(confused)

But I'm a print-line operator.

JACK

Pay attention, me old son—I don't need no print-line man, I need a reporter. Oh, and you'll be doing local car wrecks—take the pictures, write the story. We run a front-page photo of a car wreck every week, whether or not we actually have a car wreck.

Jack resumes GUTTING FISH. *Quoyle, watching this disgusting process, is getting queasy.*

JACK *(cont'd)*
(offers gutting knife:)

Want to pip a few?

QUOYLE

No. Thank you.

JACK

Now, when you get a slow week—no car wrecks—that's when you dip into Card's photo file, he's got some beauties. Car wrecks that make you feel something.

Jack leans in confidentially to Quoyle . . .

> JACK *(cont'd)*
>
> There's a knack to it. If there's a dark patch on the ground, it reads blood, whether it's motor oil or Diet Coke. And you want something human—a mitten, a purse, a baseball cap—lyin' in the road.

Jack gives Quoyle a little wink.

> JACK *(cont'd)*
>
> See, that's what makes it human. Makes the reader *feel*. A good wreck says to the reader: "There but for the grace of God . . ."

> QUOYLE
>
> Mr. Buggit—Jack—I'm no reporter—

> JACK
>
> Jesus sweet Christ, you think any of them tomcods knew how to write when I hired 'em? I get a feeling about people, that's all. I predict a cockadoodle-bright future in journalism for you.

Jack RIPS THE GUTS out of a fish with particular violence. Quoyle blanches.

> JACK *(cont'd)*
>
> Read the *Gammy Bird,* that's your new bible. Tert Card will show you the ropes.

Quoyle, barely able to breathe, is trying to grasp what Jack is telling him.

> JACK *(cont'd)*
> *(musing, mostly to himself)*
>
> Do you know how fast my sister could pip herring? Thirty fish a minute—she's got a gift for it. And what's she doing now? She's on unemployment. Because the goddamn

Canada government gave fishing rights to every country on the face of the earth.

Quoyle, ashen-faced, watches Jack discard the slimy fish guts.

EXT. THE GREEN HOUSE—DAY

An OUTHOUSE *stands behind the house.* AGNIS, *alone, approaches the outhouse, holding something in her hand . . . it's the* ZIPLOC BAG *that holds her brother's ashes.*

INT. OUTHOUSE—SAME

AGNIS *enters. She stares down into the deep hole. She unzips the Ziploc Bag . . . and* POURS THE ASHES *down into the hole. We see them falling, swirling, in* SLOW MOTION. *We hear the rustle of Agnis lifting her skirts.*

AGNIS'S FACE *is impassive, as she stares out at the sea through a small crack in the outhouse wall. We* HEAR *the splatter as she voids herself.*

> AGNIS
>
> Welcome home, Guy.

INT. THE GREEN HOUSE—AFTERNOON

QUOYLE, *still in mild shock, carrying copies of the* Gammy Bird *under his arm, enters to find* AGNIS *vigorously scrubbing the walls of the house.*

> AGNIS
> *(working, not looking at him)*
> How did it go?

> QUOYLE
> Hard to say. Where's Bunny?

> AGNIS
> Did you find a job or didn't you?

QUOYLE
(heading off)
Hard to say.

EXT. BEHIND THE GREEN HOUSE—SAME

BUNNY *sits on the cold ground, working on a craft project with great care.*

QUOYLE
Hi.

She doesn't answer, working with almost eerie concentration. He sees that she's weaving a loop of reeds (which she has pulled from the ground) connected by aluminum pop tops.

QUOYLE *(cont'd)*
Is that a belt or a crown?

No answer. He's a little spooked by the intensity of her focus. Now he notices: a nearby row of soda cans, with their tops popped. He lifts one, liquid sloshes out: the cans are full.

QUOYLE *(cont'd)*
Sweetheart, sodas go flat when you open—

BUNNY
(not looking up)
This is important.

QUOYLE
(a BEAT)
Oh.

HOT DOGS ON STICKS

which AGNIS, QUOYLE, *and* BUNNY *are roasting over the rekindled* CAMPFIRE. *It is* EVENING. *Bunny is wearing the* NECKLACE *she made from the pop-top cans.*

> QUOYLE
> *(protesting)*
> How can I do it? Even if I knew the first thing about writing, which I don't. Covering *car wrecks*? I can't do that.

> AGNIS
> Why not?

> QUOYLE
> You know why not.

> AGNIS
> We face up to the things we're afraid of, because we can't go around them.

> BUNNY
> *(helpfully)*
> Petal says he's afraid of his own shadow.

> AGNIS
> *(a BEAT; looks into the fire)*
> *Her* shadow, more like.

Quoyle is about to protest . . . but he says nothing. He pensively rotates his hotdog stick in the fire.

> AGNIS *(cont'd)*
> Car wrecks are a fact of life up here. Dangerous roads.
> *(a BEAT)*
> Come winter, the drive into town'll be damn near impossible. We'll buy us a boat.

QUOYLE

(a little testy)

I already told you, I am not a water person.

There is a GUST OF WIND, and a loud MOAN from the cables. Quoyle looks up at the house.

BUNNY

It was dragged.

Quoyle looks questioningly at Bunny.

BUNNY *(cont'd)*

The house. It was dragged here.

QUOYLE

You must've had a dream, sweetie.

AGNIS

(surprised; to Bunny:)

Who told you about that?

Quoyle gives Agnis a puzzled look . . .

AGNIS *(cont'd)*

Long time ago, on Gaze Island, the old Quoyles. They couldn't make a go of it there. Lashed the house with ropes . . . and yes, dragged it. Across the ice clear to the mainland. Right here.

Quoyle is looking at Agnis in astonishment . . . then he looks at Bunny . . . then he gapes up at the house . . .

BUNNY

(nonchalant)

Dog on fire.

QUOYLE

Huh?

Agnis indicates Quoyle's hot dog, which is now IN FLAMES. Bunny laughs with delight.

EXT. FROZEN OCEAN—QUOYLE'S POINT—TWILIGHT

A vast world of white: frozen ocean, snow covered land, white sky.

The sound of MASSIVE RUMBLING; *dogs* BARKING; PEOPLE'S SHOUTING VOICES, *wracked with exertion, shrill with urgency.*

Then, moving into this still whiteness, a tight group of MEN'S AND WOMEN'S FACES, *straining under ropes. The giant load they're pulling rumbles past, too close to identify. Ice sprays up around fir-tree rollers carrying the load.*

The Men and Women strain under their load, moving away . . . and now we see that they are dragging a HOUSE: *a huge, gaunt green house, moving like a ship, the ice cracking in its wake.*

CUT TO:

INT. GREEN HOUSE—BEDROOM—MORNING

Quoyle's eyes snap open. He stares straight ahead, almost as if he's still seeing his dream.

INT. QUOYLE'S STATION WAGON—MORNING

AGNIS *is driving;* QUOYLE, *next to her, is reading a copy of the* GAMMY BIRD. *They both have mugs of tea. Quoyle's lunchbox is at his side.* BUNNY *is in the backseat, dressing her* BABY DOLL *and* WHISPERING *to it in scolding tones.*

QUOYLE
(to Agnis)

Listen to the "News of Your Neighbors" column.

(reading from newspaper:)

"Well, we see the postman has landed in the clink for throwing the mail in Killick-Claw Harbor. He said he had too much to deliver, and folks could just take a dip and help themselves. Guess it helps if you can swim!"

He looks up at Agnis for a reaction, but she's looking straight ahead at the road.

> QUOYLE *(cont'd)*
> *(continues reading)*
> "A snowmobile mishap has taken the life of 78-year-old Caleb Boggars, whose machine fell through the ice. A well-known local electrician and accordion player, Mr. Boggars had served four years in the 1970s . . .
> *(lowering his voice:)*
> . . . for sexual assault on his daughters. We're betting they didn't cry too hard at the funeral!"

Agnis just keeps driving.

> QUOYLE *(cont'd)*
> How am I supposed to write like this? This is professional stuff.

> BUNNY
> You can't write? You're dumb.

> AGNIS
> Here now, Miss! Don't ever let me hear you talk to your father like that again.

> BUNNY
> *(defensive)*
> Petal says Dad's dumb.

> QUOYLE
> *(conciliatory)*
> All people are dumb sometimes.

Agnis gives Quoyle a look, amazed by his conciliatory, almost apologetic tone.

INT. THE GAMMY BIRD—MORNING

QUOYLE *enters, nervously clutching his lunchbox like a boy on the first day of school. He is immediately startled by a* VIOLENT

BANGING SOUND. *Quoyle flinches and crouches, as if in the line of gunfire. Then he sees that* NUTBEEM, *at his desk right beside Quoyle, is* VIOLENTLY BANGING *the top of his* BUZZING SHORTWAVE RADIO *with his fist—until the radio's* BUZZING STOPS. *Nutbeem speaks with a British accent:*

> NUTBEEM
> *(off Quoyle's alarmed expression)*
> Right. So sorry. Desperate times, desperate measures. You must be Quoyle.
> *(shakes Quoyle's hand)*
> B. Beaufield Nutbeem. I head up the Foreign News Department.

Quoyle, bemused, glances at the radio.

> CARD (O.S.)
> *(cranky, as always)*
> He steals every story off that shortwave . . .

INCLUDE TERT CARD *emerging from Jack Buggit's office from which Jack is once again absent).*

> NUTBEEM
> Which Card takes the liberty of rewriting in his own mystical tongue.

> CARD
> *(affronted)*
> Only to save you from charges of plagiarism!

Nutbeem, giving Quoyle a meaningful glance, opens a folder:

> NUTBEEM
> My story: "Burmese sawmill owners and the Rangoon Corporation met Tuesday to discuss marketing of tropical hardwood.
> *(turns the page)*

Card's rewrite: "Burnoosed sawbill awnings and the Ranger Competition met Wednesday to discuss marking of optical hairwood.

Quoyle is bewildered. Tert smiles, with a certain sadistic relish.

> ### NUTBEEM *(cont'd)*
> You're wondering, Quoyle—why does Jack Buggit allow these typographical horrors?
> *(confidentially:)*
> He feels they give humor to the paper.

> ### CARD
> *(proud, defiant)*
> People like figuring 'em out—Jack says they're better than a crossword puzzle!

The door opens, and BILLY PRETTY *enters for the day's work, struggling with a stuck zipper on his parka.*

> ### NUTBEEM
> *(introducing him to Quoyle:)*
> Mr. Billy Pretty, an old fish dog, and local landmark. Edits the Home News Page—poems, baby photos, household tips. He also writes under the pseudonym Junior Sugg for the "News of Your Neighbors" column, which is pretty much straight libel.

> ### QUOYLE
> *(intrigued, to Billy)*
> *You* write "News of Your Neighbors"?

> ### BILLY
> *(looks up from his stuck zipper; defensive:)*
> Somebody's got to.

> ### QUOYLE
> I'm a big fan.

This stops everyone cold: is Quoyle serious?

They see that he's utterly sincere. After a moment:

> CARD
> *(pointing)*
> There's your desk, Quoyle.

The "desk" is half a filing cabinet covered with a square of plywood, graced by a 1983 Ontario phone book and an ancient Smith-Corona TYPEWRITER.

> QUOYLE
> Is there a computer?

> CARD
> D'ya see one?

> QUOYLE
> *(timidly)*
> The other desks have computers . . .

> CARD
> Keen observational powers. I can understand why Jack snatched ya off the job market.

The PHONE RINGS. *Card answers it:*

> CARD *(cont'd)*
> *Gammy Bird.*
> *(listens; then, to Quoyle:)*
> You lead a charmed life, Quoyle. Two minutes on the job, already got your first car wreck.

Quoyle's eyes widen with fear.

EXT. A SCENE OF HIGHWAY CARNAGE—DAY

We open with a P.O.V. through a CAMERA VIEWFINDER. *The* CAMERA *is searching through the* BURNED WRECKAGE *of a horrible accident . . . until it* FINDS, *at the edge of the road: a solitary, blood-spattered* MAN'S BOOT.

We hear the CAMERA SHUTTER CLICK, *and see a* FLASH.
ANGLE: BILLY PRETTY *taking the picture. Meanwhile:*

QUOYLE, *nearby, writes in his notebook while a* GARRULOUS,
ELDERLY POLICE OFFICER *gives him information:*

> POLICE OFFICER
>
> Rate of speed we estimate at 65, so there's nothin' unlawful
> here. Not a whole lot you can do when a moose decides to
> get in your way.

*Quoyle, looking very queasy, flicks his glance toward the charred
wreckage—then immediately looks away from it.*

> POLICE OFFICER *(cont'd)*
> *(shakes his head)*
> The driver most likely had his chest crushed before the car
> hit the water, so at least that's a mercy—

Quoyle turns away and vomits.

> POLICE OFFICER *(cont'd)*
> *(unfazed)*
> Yar. You need a tissue?

*Quoyle, finished vomiting, can't help taking one more compulsive
glance over at the charred wreckage . . .*

QUOYLE'S P.O.V.:

PETAL'S LEGS *hang lifelessly out of a window of the wrecked
vehicle; we recognize her glittery stiletto-heeled sandals and the
bottom fringe of her crimson dress.*

QUOYLE *looks away, and accepts a tissue from the Police Officer.*

INT. QUOYLE'S STATION WAGON—DAY

QUOYLE *(wiping his lips with the tissue) is driving, with* BILLY
riding shotgun.

BILLY

It's wrecks like that one that sells papers. Jack knows his readers. Mind you there's more people down under these waters than gets killed on the roads.

(word to the wise)

You'll want to get yourself a nice little boat before long. Something that fits the water.

Quoyle sees something up ahead, on the other side of the road:

THE SAME HONEY-HAIRED MOTHER (WAVEY PROWSE) *and her vacantly smiling* SON *that he saw on the ferry. They're walking on the other side of the road, hand-in-hand, in their slickers and boots.*

QUOYLE

Who is that?

BILLY

Why?

QUOYLE

She . . . has good posture.

He tries, unsuccessfully, to cancel the stupid remark:

QUOYLE *(cont'd)*

What I mean is, she has a good stride. I mean, tall. She seems tall.

BILLY

It was grief caused her boy to be not right. She was carrying him when her husband went down at sea. Like I was saying, there's more life lost that way . . . We should of give her a ride, boy.

QUOYLE

She was going the other way.

50

BILLY
You could of turned around.

EXT. GREEN HOUSE—EARLY EVENING

QUOYLE *arrives back at the house.* AGNIS *stands at the back of a* RENTED TRUCK, *sorting through materials in the payload: thick cloth, odd mechanical devices, spools of heavy thread.* BUNNY *is playing with a length of heavy thread, carefully using it to make a new* NECKLACE *out of the* SODA POP-TOPS *(to replace the necklace she made with dandelion stems, which are by now rotting and falling apart).*

AGNIS
How was your first day?

Quoyle gives her a look: don't ask. He walks to the truck, looks in.

QUOYLE
Hi, sweetheart.

Bunny, working on her replacement necklace, doesn't answer.

QUOYLE *(cont'd)*
(puzzled by truck and its contents; to Agnis:)
What *is* all this?

AGNIS
Nephew, we can't fix up the house proper on a journalist's wages. So I have un-retired.

QUOYLE
(a BEAT)
From what?

AGNIS
Boat upholstery.
(needling him)
All us Quoyles have a feeling for boats.

                        QUOYLE
                 (with mild irritation)
Not all.

The sudden sound of FOOTSTEPS *from above makes Quoyle look up sharply, to see:*

DENNIS BUGGIT, *a muscular but boyish man in a toolbelt, climbing down a ladder from the roof of the house. He waves a greeting and hops down the last six feet to the ground.*

                        AGNIS
This is Dennis Buggit, master carpenter.

                        DENNIS
Only till I get my lobster license. I'm a fisherman in my soul.

Dennis gives Quoyle a strong, eager handshake.

                        QUOYLE
Buggit, huh? Any relation to my boss on the Gammy Bird?

Dennis's grin fades, awkwardly.

                        DENNIS
Mm-hm, yeah. My dad.

Quoyle sees that he has touched a sore spot. Dennis changes the subject:

                     DENNIS *(cont'd)*
Tomorrow I'll run 2-by-4s under your second story. I was you, I wouldn't sleep in the upstairs tonight. 'Less you wanna wake up downstairs with a thud.

INT. GREEN HOUSE—LIVING ROOM—LATE NIGHT

AGNIS *softly snores in the corner.*

BUNNY, *wide awake with anxiety, clutches Quoyle's sleeve as he sleeps. She worriedly watches his chest rise and fall.*

Bunny looks up at a WINDOW.

BUNNY'S P.O.V.: Unearthly tendrils of FOG *drift past in eerie moonglow wisps.*

Suddenly, two FACES *seem to appear out of the glowing fog: a* FERAL WHITE DOG—*and beside it, an* OLD MAN'S FACE, *an impossibly skinny, grizzled* GHOST, *eyes* FLASHING *crazy.*

BUNNY SCREAMS—*and the ghostly faces* RECEDE *into the fog.*

>   QUOYLE
>   *(waking up, groggy)*
> What . . . ?

>   BUNNY
>   *(fearful whisper)*
> A ghost. The window. A skinny ghost. And a white dog.

>   QUOYLE
>   *(hugs her)*
> Okay, sweetheart, okay.

>   BUNNY
> I didn't dream it. Don't say I did.

Quoyle is hugging her tightly, stroking her hair.

>   QUOYLE
> I won't.

INT. THE GAMMY BIRD—DAY

QUOYLE *is TYPING on his ancient Smith Corona, pausing every now and then to unjam a jammed key.*

NUTBEEM *is hunched over his shortwave radio;* BILLY *is thumbing through a book of "101 Favorite Whalemeat Recipes."*

CARD, *in Jack's office, finishes up a phone call and emerges into the newsroom:*

>   CARD
> That was Mr. Jack Buggit on the line. Won't be in till this afternoon.

>   NUTBEEM
> Migraine?

>   BILLY
> Sciatica?

>   CARD
> "Pink Eye," says he.

Card strides over to Quoyle's desk:

>   CARD *(cont'd)*
> How's your car wreck coming, Quoyle?

Card is astonished to see a sheaf of typed pages: it's at least 20 PAGES LONG.

>   CARD *(cont'd)*
>   *(picks up sheaf of pages)*
> If I wanted "War and Peace," I would of hired William Bloody Shakespeare.

Card crumples Quoyle's pages and THROWS THEM IN THE WASTE BASKET. *He marches back into Jack's office and shuts the door.*

Quoyle just sits there, like a wounded schoolboy.

NUTBEEM
(trying to console Quoyle)
It means he feels comfortable with you.

Billy goes to the waste basket and fishes out Quoyle's pages. Billy peruses the pages, like a doctor examining a critically-ill patient. Quoyle waits, with dread, for the diagnosis.

BILLY
(quiet; trying to be gentle)
The police officer had breakfast at the Codcake Diner before arriving at the accident scene?

QUOYLE
(a worried guess:)
I spelled "Codcake" wrong?

EXT. DOWN THE ROAD FROM THE GAMMY BIRD—DAY

QUOYLE *and* BILLY *are walking down the road, Billy lecturing passionately:*

BILLY
Your spelling's okay, and I've seen plenty worse grammar. But finding the center of your story, the beatin' heart of it—*that's* what makes a reporter. You oughta start by making up headlines. Short, punchy. Dramatic.
(points to horizon)
What do you see? Tell me the headline.

Quoyle peers uncertainly at the DARKENING HORIZON. *Then:*

QUOYLE
"Horizon Fills With Dark Clouds."

Billy vigorously shakes his head no.

BILLY
"Impending Storm Threatens Village!"

Quoyle just gapes at Billy.

QUOYLE

Well but . . . what if no storm comes?

BILLY

"Village Spared From Deadly Storm!"

Quoyle nods slowly, awestruck by this man's genius . . .

QUOYLE

Wow. Yeah.

Billy walks on. Quoyle lingers a moment, marveling:

QUOYLE *(cont'd)*
(to himself, savoring it:)
Village Spared From Deadly Storm.

EXT. DAYCARE CENTER—AFTERNOON

It's a daycare center in a private residence. A DOZEN LITTLE
KIDS *are running around, having a ball.*

Quoyle's station wagon pulls up. QUOYLE *and* BUNNY, *both quite
nervous, climb out.*

BUNNY

I don't wanna go here.

Quoyle gives Bunny a candy bar, and opens one for himself.

QUOYLE

Come on, sweetie.

She grimly chomps on the candy bar, makes no move to go with him.

QUOYLE *(cont'd)*
(re: the kids)
Looks like they're having fun.

                    BUNNY
Why can't I just go to work with you?

                    QUOYLE
Let's just look around, okay?

                    BUNNY
                (shrugs: suit yourself)
I'm not gonna talk to anybody.

A YOUNG WOMAN *is chasing around with the rollicking kids . . .
and then Quoyle sees, under a tree:*

WAVEY PROWSE, *combing the hair of her vacant-faced son,*
HERRY.

*Quoyle watches her, summoning his courage. He hastily wraps his
candy bar, puts it in his pocket, and leads Bunny into the yard
toward Wavey and Herry:*

                    QUOYLE
                (nervous, blurting out)
Hi there—it's our first day. She's in the after-school
program—

                    BUNNY
                (to Quoyle)
I don't like these kids.

                    QUOYLE
Bunny—

                    BUNNY
They're boring! Boring boring boring—

                    QUOYLE
                (sharply)
That's enough.
                (embarrassed, to Wavey)
She's not usually like this.

But Wavey is not at all fazed by Bunny's behavior.

> WAVEY
>
> Not usually like what?
> *(casually to Bunny)*
> I hate going to new places where I don't know anybody.

Bunny, caught off-guard by this woman's matter-of-fact acceptance, eyes Wavey warily. Then:

> BUNNY
> *(re: Herry)*
> What's wrong with him?

> QUOYLE
>
> Bunny, that's not nice. There's nothing wrong with—

> WAVEY
> *(to Bunny)*
> Sure there is. This is Herry.
> *(kneels down beside Bunny)*
> When he was being born, he didn't get enough air to breathe.

Quoyle, speechless, observes the direct, clear-eyed way that Wavey is able to talk to Bunny.

> WAVEY *(cont'd)*
>
> And that made him a little slower than most people. What's your name?

> BUNNY
>
> Bunny.

> WAVEY
>
> Hm. A bunny rabbit.

> BUNNY
> *(a BEAT)*
> That's what my mother calls me.

WAVEY

Is Mommy at work now?

BUNNY

She's asleep, with the angels.

Wavey takes in this information without comment.

BUNNY *(cont'd)*
(impulsive, a bit defiant)

I *am* a Bunny Rabbit.

Bunny begins to HOP AROUND *like a bunny.*

WAVEY

You certainly are.

Herry LAUGHS *with delight. He starts* HOPPING AROUND *like
a super-charged pogo stick. Bunny and Herry hop off together.*

*Wavey stands up. Quoyle is alone with her now. She looks at him
with her clear eyes. She's as comfortable in silence as Quoyle is
agonized. He nervously tries to start a conversation:*

QUOYLE

Which one of those women is in charge here?

*He's indicating the two women running around after the frolicking
kids.*

WAVEY

Neither of 'em. They're just moms.

*Quoyle sees a kid bump into a crafts table, knocking a pair of
scissors to the floor.*

QUOYLE

Somebody should be being paying more attention, huh?
Kids running around, scissors on the floor . . .

Wavey, unblinking, just looks at him.

> QUOYLE *(cont'd)*
> I mean, shouldn't somebody be supervising . . .

Her gaze is steady, botomless. He is in the dawning panic of beginning to realize . . .

> WAVEY
> Well. I better get back to work. Supervising and all.

Quoyle is dying a slow death.

> WAVEY *(cont'd)*
> I'm Wavey Prowse, I run the place.
> *(glances at kids, dryly:)*
> They *are* having entirely too much fun, aren't they. It's a constant problem around here.

She heads off with a cool graceful stride.

INT. STATION WAGON—DAY

Quoyle drives, alone. He shakes his head in self-disgust . . .

> QUOYLE
> *(murmurs to himself)*
> "Bumbling Dad Humiliated in Daycare."

INT. SKIPPER WILL'S DINER—DAY

QUOYLE *enters, with a* COMPUTER PRINTOUT *in hand. He approaches the counter and sits down at the end, apart from the other customers. He eyes the display of pies with great interest.*

> NUTBEEM (O.S.)
> Quoyle!

Quoyle looks up, sees NUTBEEM *and* DENNIS *sitting at a booth. Nutbeem vigorously waves Quoyle over.*

DENNIS
C'mon over, Quoyle!

Quoyle smiles slightly, surprised and flattered by the invitation. He goes over to Nutbeem and Dennis's booth, sits down. They're eating SQUIDBURGERS *(with tentacles dangling from the sides of the buns).*

NUTBEEM
(re: computer printout)
Ah, you've been to the harbormaster.

QUOYLE
(nods, re: the printout)
Boats in, boats out.

NUTBEEM
(dryly)
Not exactly the stuff of legends, eh?

Quoyle nods worriedly.

NUTBEEM *(cont'd)*
(words of advice:)
Sometimes there's a story behind the story.

DENNIS
Have you got a boat for yourself yet, Quoyle?
(before Quoyle can answer)
Y'oughta get Alvin Yark to build you one.
(devilish smile)
Or you could buy Nutbeem's.

Nutbeem smiles: the joke's on him.

NUTBEEM
(explains to Quoyle)
I built a Chinese junk. Sailed it up from Brazil.

Unfortunately I missed Manhattan by a mile or so. And got stranded here when I shipwrecked by Gaze Island.

Nutbeem shrugs: easy come, easy go.

NUTBEEM *(cont'd)*

I've almost finished my repairs. I'll be sailing away soon.

(confidentially)

She's ugly. And the only thing I've ever loved.

Dennis rises.

DENNIS

Your story tugs at me bladder.

Dennis heads off toward the Men's Room, but just now JACK *happens to enter the diner, with a load of* FISH *he has caught—father and son are accidentally too close together to ignore each other. There's a moment of terrible, wordless tension.*

After a moment, Jack stiffly nods hello, and Dennis nods back, not quite looking at his father. Jack brusquely moves past Dennis to the counter. Dennis continues on into the Men's Room.

Quoyle, having observed this tense encounter, leans toward Nutbeem:

QUOYLE

What's the problem between 'em?

Quoyle and Nutbeem's eyes meet. The Brit sighs.

NUTBEEM

First thing: you have to understand about the curse.

Quoyle's intrigued.

Nutbeem hesitates: should he tell it? Quoyle makes a rolling hand motion, hurry it up.

62

NUTBEEM *(cont'd)*
Jack Buggit's father, his grandfather, his great-
grandfather—they all died at sea.

Quoyle nods: go on, tell it.

NUTBEEM *(cont'd)*
Second thing: Jack is sensitive. Especially about the sea.
(off Quoyle's puzzled reaction:)
Sensitive. That's what they call people around here who . . .
know things.

QUOYLE
(dubious)
You mean like psychic things?

Nutbeem nods.

QUOYLE *(cont'd)*
(a prompt)
And . . . ?

NUTBEEM
Alright. Dennis's older brother Jesson, everyone's favorite.
Goes to sea like his dad. One day, the rest of the family's
sitting by the radio, and Jack goes white . . .

Quoyle listens intently.

NUTBEEM *(cont'd)*
He stands up and announces, "Jesson is gone." And walks
out of the house. Grief too big for walls to hold it.

Nutbeem runs a finger down the frost on his beer mug.

NUTBEEM *(cont'd)*
So Dennis is forbidden the sea. But being free, Newfie, and
twenty-one, he goes anyway.

QUOYLE

And that's enough to—?

NUTBEEM

Death storm. A monster wave *cracks* her steel hull
amidships, a one inch crack from starboard to port. Men go
in the water. Dennis is lost. After a week . . .

Quoyle puts down his squidburger, listening . . .

NUTBEEM *(cont'd)*

They come to Jack and tell him the search has been called
off. He stands like a stone. Then he turns, sharp, the way he
does. Says only, "He's alive. And I know where."

Quoyle is rapt.

NUTBEEM *(cont'd)*

He goes to sea, alone, in just a skiff—and *finds* Dennis
washed ashore, in a cove. Can you guess the odds? Finds
him. Finds him. Both arms broken, ninety-nine percent
dead.

Nutbeem leans in close.

NUTBEEM *(cont'd)*

The boy comes to. Jack says, "If you ever step in a boat
again, I'll drown ya m'self." And you know what the kid
said . . . ?

*Quoyle spots JACK making his way through the diner toward their
table.*

QUOYLE

Say it fast.

NUTBEEM

He says, "Fishing licenses are all spoken for, I'd appreciate you givin' me yours." Jack looked in his eyes. They never spoke again.

> JACK
> *(approaching their table)*
> Quoyle—ya got the Shipping News written up yet?

Quoyle pulls a folded, typewritten page from his pocket and hands it to Jack.

Jack peruses the page with a critical squint. Then:

> JACK *(cont'd)*
> There's nothin' here.

Quoyle swallows hard.

> QUOYLE
> Ships in, ships out. What else is there?

> JACK
> If I knew, I'd write it myself.
> *(a growl)*
> I took a chance on ya, Quoyle—don't let me down.

Quoyle is flummoxed. Jack strides away and exits the diner.

Nutbeem gives Quoyle a sad, sympathetic little smile.

INT. GREEN HOUSE BEDROOM—NIGHT

COLD RAIN *is leaking in through the incompletely patched ceiling.* QUOYLE *and* BUNNY *lie awake in their cold, rain-soaked sleeping bags. The* CABLES ARE MOANING HORRIBLY *in the fierce wind. Bunny's teeth are chattering.*

> BUNNY
> I wanna go home.

He nods with understanding. He reaches over and hugs her.

> BUNNY *(cont'd)*
> Don't do that. Don't touch me!

AGNIS, *visible in the bedroom directly across the hall, is awakened by Bunny's angry voice. Quoyle, startled and confused, stops hugging Bunny.*

> AGNIS
> You woke me up.

> BUNNY
> I don't care I don't care—

> AGNIS
> Stop that, child.

> BUNNY
> You're not my mommy!

Bunny starts SCREAMING *at Agnis: an* INCOHERENT, ANGRY YELLING THAT GOES ON AND ON.

Quoyle tries to hug Bunny and shush her, but she pushes him away and keeps YELLING, *blotting out any possibility of conversation.*

> AGNIS
> *(shouting to be heard; to Quoyle)*
> You going to let her carry on like that?

Quoyle nervously hugs Bunny, trying to shush her, stroking her hair:

> QUOYLE
> Alright, sweetie, alright . . .

He unwraps a candy bar that he has kept next to his sleeping bag. Bunny eats the candy, quieting down.

Agnis shakes her head in silent disapproval of Quoyle's parenting style.

                    QUOYLE *(cont'd)*
                    (frustrated, to Agnis:)
Well what do you want me to do? How are we supposed to
live in this place anyway? If you hadn't dragged us up to
this frozen dump, we wouldn't be—

                    AGNIS
                    (stern)
She's got an excuse for her everlasting whining—she's six
years old. You're supposed to be a man.

Quoyle and Bunny are both sobered by Agnis's intensity.

                    AGNIS *(cont'd)*
Act like one, or get out. Your choice.

Quoyle, chastened, considers what his aunt just said . . . and we:

                                          CUT TO:

EXT. KILLICK-CLAW DOCK—DAY

QUOYLE *is walking carefully around a small* BOAT, *hauled up
beside packing crates and garbage at the end of the wharf. The boat
has a* "FOR SALE" *sign.*

*Quoyle runs his hand along the rail. He takes a deep breath,
gathering his manly determination.*

But then Quoyle is distracted from his mission by the SOUND OF
A MAN AND WOMAN ARGUING—*coming from an impressive*
BOTTERJACHT *farther down the dock.*

EXT. DOCK—THE BOTTERJACHT—A BIT LATER

QUOYLE *hesitantly approaches the Botterjacht. He inspects the
beautifully detailed teakwood railing.*

> BAYONET (O.S.)
>> *(sharply)*
> Do I know you?

Quoyle looks up ahead to the bow, where a rolling bar has been set up. BAYONET MELVILLE *is mixing drinks. He's a dapper man with a florid face, jaded eyes, and shocking white hair.*

> QUOYLE
>> *(tentative)*
> Newspaper. Reporter . . . I'm a reporter. Wanted to see . . . this your boat?

> BAYONET
>> *(points to a dilapidated boat nearby:)*
> *That* is a boat.
>> *(points to her own deck:)*
> *This* a Botterjacht.

Nearby SILVER MELVILLE, *a faded beauty in a silk robe, glances disdainfully at Quoyle above her gimlet.*

> BAYONET *(cont'd)*
> She was built for Hitler. He was the original owner.

> QUOYLE
> *Adolf* Hitler?

> SILVER
>> *(rolls her eyes)*
> No, Bruce Hitler.

Quoyle smiles foolishly, absorbing the insult. He takes out his reporter's notebook.

> QUOYLE
> If I could just ask you a few—

BAYONET

Finest botterjacht ever built in Holland. Flat-bottomed—she
can go right up on shore in a storm. Incredibly heavy, forty
tons of oak—

SILVER

(weary, impatient)

Tell him what happened in Hurricane Bob.

Baronet looks at his wife; it's clear they hate each other. She nods:
go on, tell it.

MELVILLE

The waves kept shoving her onto the beach. She pounded
twelve beach houses, expensive ones, to rubble.

SILVER

(angry and drunk)

WHAMM!

(to Melville:)

Now tell them who let our insurance lapse.

Silence.

SILVER *(cont'd)*

It took six very expensive lawyers to weasel us out of it. An
inch from bankruptcy.

She winks:

SILVER *(cont'd)*

Moral of the story? When you marry a tour guide, confine
his authority to mixing the drinks.

She steps into the cabin and SLAMS the door behind her.

QUOYLE

Did I . . . come at a bad time?

Bayonet laughs cynically.

> BAYONET
> Yes. Ten years ago would've been better.

EXT. ROAD—LATE AFTERNOON

QUOYLE *is driving his wagon, alone, pensive.* A DRIZZLE *is falling. He's headed for the* GAMMY BIRD OFFICE, *right down the street.*

> QUOYLE
> "Wife Fires Heavy Artillery Aboard Hitler Boat."

Then Quoyle sees up ahead: WAVEY *and* HERRY *in their rain slickers, walking hand-in-hand just like before. This time, Quoyle does pull over . . .*

> QUOYLE *(cont'd)*
> Give you folks a lift?

> WAVEY
> Hi. Thanks, but—Herry likes to walk.

> QUOYLE
> *(nervous, abrupt)*
> It's a nice day for walking.

Wavey is thrown off. Quoyle immediately realizes he just made an idiotic remark: the only sound, besides the POURING RAIN, *is the* THWACK-THWACKING OF *Quoyle's* WINDSHIELD WIPERS, *as if they were mocking him.*

> WAVEY
> Mr. Quoyle, about the other day. I'm sorry we got off on the wrong foot—

> QUOYLE
> Oh no no, I was way off base. I admire anybody who works with kids. Toughest job in the world.

She smiles, but only slightly. Quoyle feels uncomfortable—and as usual, he impulsively gropes to fill the silence:

> QUOYLE *(cont'd)*
>
> I'm a journalist myself.

> WAVEY
> *(intrigued)*
>
> Really.

Quoyle nods vigorously.

> WAVEY *(cont'd)*
> *(confidentially)*
>
> Have you seen our local paper?
> Strictly fish wrap.

Quoyle goes pale. He doesn't know what to say.

> WAVEY *(cont'd)*
>
> What?

> QUOYLE
>
> I'm . . . the new reporter there.

> WAVEY
> *(caught off-guard)*
>
> Oh . . .
> *(observing Quoyle's discomfort)*
> Well. I'm sure you'll . . . elevate the level of journalism . . .

> QUOYLE
> *(weakly)*
>
> Nice to see you. Bye now.

Quoyle smiles stupidly and drives off toward the Gammy Bird.

Wavey sighs: poor Quoyle. She takes Herry's hand and continues walking.

EXT. FRONT OF GAMMY BIRD—MOMENTS LATER

QUOYLE *parks his car, glumly shuffles into the office.*

INT. GAMMY BIRD OFFICE—SAME

as QUOYLE *enters, finds Nutbeem listening to the shortwave. (In b.g., through the window to Jack's office, we see* CARD *and* BILLY *struggling to fix a broken Mr. Coffee machine, quietly arguing about how to do it.*

> QUOYLE
> *(to Nutbeem, with dread)*
> Did you read it?

> NUTBEEM
> Hm? Oh—yes.

Nutbeem picks up TYPED PAGES, *which he has* HEAVILY EDITED IN RED INK.

> QUOYLE
> How bad is it?

> NUTBEEM
> It's not. It's almost good, actually.
> Is this true—this yarn about her getting caught in Hurricane Bob?
> *(amused)*
> She accidentally smashed six other boats to matchsticks . . . ?

> QUOYLE
> *(nods)*
> And came out with barely a scratch.
> Hitler had her built for punishment.

> NUTBEEM
> This belongs right under your lead.

Quoyle distractedly glances out the window at the FIGURE OF WAVEY IN THE DISTANCE, *walking with Herry.*

> NUTBEEM *(cont'd)*
> Excellent posture.

Quoyle is puzzled at first . . . then Nutbeem indicates he's talking about the distant figure of Wavey. Quoyle is taken aback.

> NUTBEEM *(cont'd)*
> People talk.

INT. THE GREEN HOUSE—EVENING

As QUOYLE *enters the house, he notices that a long piece of* TWINE *has been placed in the doorway.* INTRICATE KNOTS *have been tied along its length. Odd, meticulous work. Quoyle doesn't know quite what to make of it.*

Then he hears a HAMMERING *sound from upstairs.*

> QUOYLE
> *(calls out)*
> Dennis?

INT. UPSTAIRS IN THE GREEN HOUSE—SAME

QUOYLE *comes up the stairs, and sees that it's* not *Dennis who's hammering—it's* BUNNY, HAMMERING THE HEAD OF HER BABY DOLL, *wielding a carpenter's hammer with both hands.*

> QUOYLE
> Bunny, what are you doing?

> BUNNY
> *(re: doll)*
> She's boring.

Quoyle kneels down beside her. He watches with deep concern as Bunny hammers the doll.

EXT. BEHIND THE GREEN HOUSE—EVENING

A clear, chilly evening. AGNIS *is sitting on a rock, facing the ocean, with a tea mug, a bottle of Bushmill's, and a small, well-worn* LEATHERBOUND BOOK. *Her eyes are glistening with sadness as she reads the book.*

QUOYLE *approaches.*

> QUOYLE
> How was Bunny when you picked her up from daycare?

> AGNIS
> Alright.
> *(a BEAT)*
> A little snotty.

Quoyle sees the sad gleam in Agnis's eyes.

> QUOYLE
> *(indicates her leatherbound book)*
> What's that?

Agnis closes the book, as if to say: none of your business. She looks up at Quoyle. Then:

> AGNIS
> *(reciting from memory)*
> "Auld Nature swears, the lovely dears / Her noblest work she classes, O: / Her 'prentice han' she tried on man, / An' then she made the lasses, O."

Quoyle stares blankly at her.

> AGNIS *(cont'd)*
> Robert Burns.

Quoyle thinks about it a moment.

QUOYLE
(re: the book)
Somebody gave you that?

She nods. He studies her.

QUOYLE *(cont'd)*
Somebody you're missing.

Agnis hesitates.

AGNIS
Six years ago today. Leukemia.
(a BEAT)
We weren't married. But that's just a technicality.

Quoyle nods, sympathetic. He takes a step toward her, on the verge of reaching out and giving her a comforting embrace . . .

. . . but her glance is sharp, and Quoyle stops short.

INT. GAMMY BIRD—DAY

QUOYLE *is alone in the office, pretending to peck away at a story. Actually, he's looking:*

THROUGH THE WINDOW (QUOYLE'S P.O.V.)

Outside, JACK BUGGIT, TERT CARD, BILLY PRETTY *and* NUTBEEM *are all circling around a* BOAT *(the one that Quoyle saw with the "For Sale" sign on it), attached to its rented trailer. They are talking to each other in grave, learned tones.*

And then they head into the office . . .

INT. GAMMY BIRD—SAME

First through the door is TERT CARD . . .

                              CARD
    Is that your boat?

                             QUOYLE
                             (nods)
    Just bought 'er.

Card snorts and shakes his head.

Uh-oh. Quoyle looks from one face to another. Even BILLY *is
irritated.* NUTBEEM *gazes down, embarrassed for Quoyle.*

                        QUOYLE *(cont'd)*
    Well. It's a speed boat—

                              JACK
    It's a shit boat. A wallowing cockeyed bastard that'll sink
    in a bathtub.

Quoyle just blinks.

                             BILLY
    Makes you cry to look at it. When you're ready to get
    serious, I'll take you to Alvin Yark, he'll build ya a sweet
    little Rodney.

Jack shakes his head sadly:

                              JACK
    You don't have the sense God gave a doughnut, do ya?

Quoyle burns with shame.

                         JACK *(cont'd)*
    I'm goin' home.

Jack heads for the door. Then, some parting advice for Quoyle:

                         JACK *(cont'd)*
    Best you can do is bury it, some dark night.

Jack exits, shutting the door shutting with finality behind him.

> CARD
>
> What in hell is *this*?

Card holds up some sheets of paper from Quoyle's desk, along with photos of the Melvilles' botterjacht.

> CARD *(cont'd)*
> *(reading)*
> Hitler's Barge . . . ?

> QUOYLE
> *(to Card; trying to stand up to him)*
> That goes with the shipping news. Story of a vessel in port.

> CARD
> What about the motorcycle accident?

> QUOYLE
> *(nervous, with bravado)*
> I like this story better.

Billy and Nutbeem both look over at Quoyle, surprised to see a spark of independence in him. Quoyle smiles nervously.

> CARD
> So you didn't do the one Jack wanted you to do, and you did one he don't know you did!

Silence. Quoyle swallows. Card peruses the article:

> CARD *(cont'd)*
> This is worse than yer boat. If Jack even *sniffs* this, he cuts you up for lobster bait.
> *(sadistically)*
> By God, I think I'll run it.

QUOYLE
(weakly)

You will?

Card nods, relishing Quoyle's growing anxiety.

INT. QUOYLE'S STATION WAGON—DAY

QUOYLE *somberly drives through the* RAIN, *hauling the "shit boat" (which is* BUMPING AND RATTLING *in the trailer) behind his car. He glances in his* REARVIEW MIRROR, *eyeing the boat with grim regret.*

Then in the rearview mirror he SEES:

PETAL

rising to her feet in the boat, spreading her arms and luxuriating in the wind and rain, letting it toss her hair and redden her cheeks; her dress clinging to her body. She looks at Quoyle, her face confident and gleaming.

QUOYLE

stares with misery and longing.

EXT. WAVEY'S HOUSE—DAY

Quoyle's car and boat are parked in front. (The rain has stopped.)

INT. WAVEY'S LIVING ROOM—DAY

Daycare in progress. The comfy room has been given over to the KIDS, *who are playing various games, romping, play-acting, etc. (A wall of Polaroids of each child faces a map of Newfoundland with drawings of moose and lobster.)*

QUOYLE *enters, looks around . . .*

. . . and then sees BUNNY, *over in a corner looking at a book with* HERRY—*the two of them apart from the other children.*

BUNNY
(quietly to rapt Herry)
. . . and he made a cocoon, which is like a house, except it's for a caterpillar.

QUOYLE
(approaches)
Hi—

BUNNY
Shh. I'm reading.

QUOYLE
(confused)
Reading?

BUNNY
(whisper to Quoyle; re: Herry)
He thinks I know how.

Quoyle nods: your secret is safe with me.

INT. THE LIVING ROOM—LATER

QUOYLE, *with* BUNNY *astride his back, rampages around on all fours,* SNORTING *like a pig.* OTHER KIDS *are squealing, delighted, making excited little runs at the "pig," swatting him with throw pillows and sweaters.*

WAVEY *comes through the doorway, drying her hands, just behind where* HERRY *is sitting. Quoyle doesn't see Wavey, he's thrasing and bellowing, lost in the game.*

Then Quoyle notices her. Suddenly self-conscious, he stops playing.

The kids look up at Wavey, to see whether she's going to scold them. Then:

WAVEY
(matter-of-fact, to Herry)
Go on. Get the pig.

Herry grins and dashes off to plow into the prey. Quoyle, with a grateful glance at Wavey, welcomes Herry into the game. The kids all squeal with joy as Quoyle plays the pig with renewed vigor, snorting and tickling Herry's ribs with his nose.

INT. WAVEY'S KITCHEN—A LITTLE LATER

The daycare kids have left, except for one BOY *who is being shepherded out by his* MOM.

THE MOM
'Night, Wavey.

WAVEY *is sitting at the kitchen table, working on a* BEAUTIFULLY CRAFTED HOME-MADE KITE; *she clearly has an artistic bent.*

WAVEY
(as Mom and Boy exit)
'Night, Sarah. 'Night, Patrick.

QUOYLE *is admiring a floor-to-ceiling shelf full of* BOOKS. *In b.g.* BUNNY *and* HERRY *are happily playing together.*

QUOYLE
(re: the books)
Have you read all these?

WAVEY
Only the good parts.
(not looking up from her work)
Could you hold these two pieces together for me?

QUOYLE
Oh.

He sits down and helps her with the kite. Their faces are close together.

                    WAVEY
    You need to hold the ends of the rods flush against each
    other, or else I can't fasten the cloth.

Bunny and Herry come running into the kitchen, playing with a ball.

Bunny sees a SMALL, GOSSAMER KITE *(that's already built) on the kitchen counter. She goes over and impulsively grabs it.*

                    QUOYLE
    Bunny—careful—it's fragile—

                    BUNNY
    I wanna see if it can fly!

                    QUOYLE
    No no, not in the house—

                    WAVEY
                (calmly; to Bunny)
    Throw it up in the air, high as you can, and count till it
    comes down.

Bunny stands on a chair, throws the kite, and watches it slowly flutter down.

                    BUNNY
    One, two, three, four, five, six.

The kite softly reaches the floor.

                    WAVEY
                (acting impressed)
    Have you been to flight school?

                              BUNNY
                        (pleased; earnest:)
   No. Not really.

Quoyle, impressed by Wavey's unflappable manner, is looking at her with something like awe. She glances over at him—and he immediately looks back down at the kite rods he's supposed to be holding together.

INT. THE GAMMY BIRD—DAY

Business as usual: QUOYLE *pecking out a story at his typewriter;* NUTBEEM *at the shortwave; Billy on the phone talking about a Church Bake-off.* CARD *ensconced like a king in Jack's office.*

They hear a CAR DOOR SLAM HARD. *Through the window they see* JACK BUGGIT *heading this way, a copy of the Gammy Bird tucked under his arm. He is striding briskly, his eyes ablaze with purpose.*

Card hurriedly tidies up the top of Jack's desk, races out of Jack's office—and tries to look nonchalant as JACK ENTERS.

Everyone murmurs hello to Jack . . . but he doesn't answer, just marches straight into his office.

                              JACK
                        (without looking back)
   Card.

Card looks at the others, then follows Jack into the office.

INT. JACK'S OFFICE—SAME

Jack notices a DROP OF COFFEE *on his desk mat. He looks up and fixes Card with a glare.*

                              JACK
   If you're gonna shanghai my office, Tert, you'd best conceal
   the evidence.

Tert is about to respond—but Jack dismisses the issue with a brusque wave of the hand. He's got something more important to talk about:

> JACK *(cont'd)*
> *(indicates newspaper on his desk)*
> This "Hitler Boat"—did you assign it?

> CARD
> Nope. Wasn't my idea.

INT. THE OUTER OFFICE—MOMENTS LATER

CARD *emerges and gives* QUOYLE *a tight little smile:*

> CARD
> *(to Quoyle; a death sentence:)*
> He wants *you.*

Quoyle swallows hard.

INT. JACK'S OFFICE—SAME

as QUOYLE *enters, sits down.*

> QUOYLE
> I'm—It's like I told you, Mr. Buggit, I'm not really a reporter. I just thought—I'm sorry if I—

> JACK
> *(sharply)*
> Stop flousing about.

Quoyle falls silent, slouching miserably.

> JACK *(cont'd)*
> Got four phone calls last night about the Hitler Boat. People enjoyed it. Mrs. Buggit liked it. 'Course you don't know nothin' about boats, but that's entertaining, too. So listen here, me old son, I'm giving you a weekly column.

Quoyle looks at Jack in confusion.

>   JACK *(cont'd)*
> A story about a different boat every week. Human stuff.
> Who owned the boat, who lived and died on her, who
> drowned, who was saved. Who lost his fortune. Who had
> his heart broke. You follow?

>   QUOYLE
>   *(shocked, uncomprehending)*
> You . . . thought it was okay?

>   JACK
>   *(shouts to Card:)*
> Order this boy a new computer, Tert!

ANGLE—TERT CARD,

just outside Jack's office, is thrown off by this turn of events.

>   JACK (O.S.) *(cont'd)*
> Buy him a real IBM, not one a them Japan clones—you got
> that?

Tert is too stunned to respond.

BACK WITH JACK AND QUOYLE

>   QUOYLE
>   *(overcome with emotion)*
> Mr. Buggit . . . I . . .

>   JACK
> Did I or did I not tell you my name is Jack?

>   QUOYLE
> You did.

INT. THE OUTER OFFICE—MOMENTS LATER

QUOYLE *emerges, shell-shocked.* NUTBEEM *gives him an encouraging nod;* BILLY*'s eyes twinkle.*

> QUOYLE
> *(to Card; very quietly)*
> Computer. IBM.

> CARD
> *(snarls)*
> Get back to work.

INT. GREEN HOUSE—BEDROOM—NIGHT

The sleeping bags have been replaced by twin beds pushed right next to each other. BUNNY, *asleep, is clutching Quoyle's sleeve for security.* QUOYLE *is wide awake (in his bed next to Bunny's), marvelling at the events of the day. After a long moment, he murmurs to himself:*

> QUOYLE
> "Imbecile Does Something Right, Stuns Crowd."

EXT. AGNIS'S SHOP—DAY

QUOYLE *parks his station wagon and heads into the shop.*

INT. AGNIS'S SHOP—DAY

QUOYLE *enters, looks around at the racks of leathers and fabrics and the billowing sailcloth hung over the windows.*

AGNIS *is working with* MAVIS BANGS, *a clear-eyed woman in her 60s; they're busily stretching a piece of leather upholstery.*

> QUOYLE
> *(excitedly)*
> Aunt, guess what—

AGNIS
(busy; to Mavis)
Let's pull it a wee bit tighter.
(to Quoyle)
This is my assistant, Mavis Bangs.

Quoyle nods hello to Mavis. Then, impatiently:

QUOYLE
Aunt, I'm gonna have my own column—

AGNIS
(to Mavis, re: the upholstery)
I'll hold, you clamp.
(to Quoyle; distractedly)
What, Nephew?

Agnis and Mavis continue to work with intense focus; they're a good team.

QUOYLE
Did you read my article about the Hitler Boat?

Suddenly Agnis and Mavis stop working. They exchange a glance.

QUOYLE *(cont'd)*
What.

AGNIS
Silver and Bayonet Melville were clients of mine. They
pulled anchor last night. Without paying a penny for all the
work we did for 'em.

This news catches Quoyle by surprise.

MAVIS
(to Quoyle)
You find out where they went, we'll give you the Pulitzer.

EXT. HILLSIDE—DAY

Billowy clouds frame a sleek KITE *darting this way and that.*

> WAVEY (O.S.)
> *(shouting)*
> Herry Prowse! Look how well your kite is doing!

We SEE *Wavey now, seated atop a grassy slope. It is she who holds the string;* HERRY *is way down at the bottom of the hill with* BUNNY—*who is teaching him how to make necklaces from wildflowers.*

> WAVEY *(cont'd)*
> *(shouting)*
> Are you making it dance with your thoughts?

On this he looks up. Serious.

> WAVEY *(cont'd)*
> *(shouting)*
> Keep thinking your thoughts! Your kite is doing *so* much better than Mr. Quoyle's!

REVEAL *that* QUOYLE *has been sitting right beside Wavey all along. He holds the string of a big, glum kite that hangs motionless in space with barely a flutter. As she watches the kids, he stares at her, deciding whether to ask . . .*

> QUOYLE
> *(barely audible)*
> Do you think Bunny's . . . strange?
> *(a BEAT)*
> Mentally.

Wavey looks over . . . and sees that he's worried half to death.

> WAVEY
> The Skinny Ghost? With the White Dog?

QUOYLE

She told you about that?

Wavey nods: no big deal.

WAVEY

Maybe she's sensitive. The way some folks around here are.

Quoyle is dubious.

QUOYLE

What about the necklaces. You know how many she makes? And she . . . bashed in her baby doll's brains with a hammer.

WAVEY

A baby doll doesn't have brains. It's a toy.

But there's more:

QUOYLE

And . . . she's saving her mother a room. Did she tell you that?

Wavey's slow nod.

QUOYLE *(cont'd)*

You know stuff about kids. You have all those books.

WAVEY

The ones I read to teach Herry. They don't make me an expert—

QUOYLE
(blurting)
Just. Is she strange? Or is she okay?

That was naked. He swallows.

QUOYLE *(cont'd)*

I mean. If you had to guess.

Wavey studies him a moment, sees how deep his need is. She looks down the hill at Bunny playing with Herry. Then:

> WAVEY
> That little girl is the only friend my son ever had. So she's strange, you bet.

Wavey's eyes are steady and certain.

EXT. HEADLAND ABOVE OCEAN—DAY (LATER)

Quoyle RUNNING, *huffing, through a bog with every color of berries imaginable. Around another bend in the path. He stops, hands on his knees.*

He listens . . . and hears nothing. He's annoyed.

> QUOYLE
> *(shouting)*
> Where *are* you guys? S'posed to be chasing me!

Still nothing. He trudges back the way he came. He peeks around a bend to see . . .

. . . Bunny is teaching Herry to pick berries.

> BUNNY
> *(to Quoyle, very serious)*
> We're busy.

Quoyle slaps his hands across his mouth: sorry. He tiptoes off, rounds a bend . . . and sees:

DOWN BELOW—ON THE ROCKY SHORELINE

WAVEY *strolling by herself, carefully making her way along the rocks by the sea . . .*

EXT. DOWN ON THE SHORELINE—A BIT LATER

QUOYLE *catches up with Wavey. She smiles, says nothing. They walk together across the rocks, with piles of seaweed on the shore below them.*

WAVEY

How was hide and seek?

QUOYLE

They'd rather pick berries.

Wavey nods. Quoyle and Wavey keep walking.

Then Wavey stops, and just gazes out at the ocean.

Quoyle looks up at Wavey standing above him on the rock.

He is struck by her beauty. He just keeps staring up at her. All he wants is to hold her . . .

. . . but since she is above him on the rocks, he impulsively grabs the only part of her he can reach: her ankles. His head presses against her skirt, feeling the warmth of her legs through the fabric.

Wavey barely breathes. She closes her eyes. A long moment.

Then, when she opens her eyes again:

WAVEY
(quietly)

Do you know how he died? My husband? Herold Prowse?

Quoyle stalled, hands dangling, watches Wavey as she slides down the rock, safe now, protecting herself with her story of grief:

WAVEY *(cont'd)*

It was a calm night when Herold took the boat out. No sign of any storm.

Quoyle just listens.

> WAVEY *(cont'd)*
> Storms can be sudden around here. He wasn't the only one whose boat went down.

She's strangely cool, stating it plainly:

> WAVEY *(cont'd)*
> It's four years. And it's yesterday.

Quoyle considers this.

And they resume walking, not looking at each other.

EXT. HEATH—DAY

On the edge of the headland heath: Quoyle follows close behind Wavey, climbing up the slope of the berry grounds.

Wavey is conscious of Quoyle behind her. She suddenly stops, turns, and faces Quoyle—very close to him.

> WAVEY
> Is it the same way for you? With your wife?

Quoyle nods, painful, yes—when suddenly and instinctively their arms go around each other. A stumbling search for a foothold—and then they are down together on the ground—letting themselves roll together, clinging, a jumble of arms and legs, faces awkwardly pressed against each other, warm skin.

A moment's stillness—only the sound of the sea and of children's voices suddenly clear—and Wavey shoves Quoyle away. She scrambles up and runs away.

Quoyle lies in the heater, watching her run away. He groans and puts his head down into the heather.

EXT. THE HEADLAND—LATER

QUOYLE, WAVEY, BUNNY, *and* HERRY *are packing up their picnic stuff, rolling up the kites, etc. Bunny and Herry are singing a* SILLY CHILDREN'S SONG; *but Wavey and Quoyle work silently. Then:*

> WAVEY
> *(quiet, to Quoyle)*
> Did I blow it? Or can you still be my friend?

> QUOYLE
> *(quiet, hoarse)*
> Your friend. Sure.

EXT. THE GREEN HOUSE—EVENING

QUOYLE *and* BUNNY *arrive back at the house. Bunny scampers inside ahead of him. Quoyle is about to enter the house, but stops when he notices: another long, intricately knotted piece of* TWINE *has been placed there. It vaguely troubles Quoyle.*

INT. UPSTAIRS BEDROOM—NIGHT

We can see that progress has been made in the renovation: windows repaired, walls patched. QUOYLE *and* BUNNY *lie in their beds. Quoyle, remembering something, reaches into his pocket and pulls out the* KNOTTED TWINE *he found earlier:*

> QUOYLE
> This yours?

Bunny, half-asleep, shakes her head no.

> BUNNY
> *(yawns drowsily)*
> The ghost brought it. Then he ran away.

QUOYLE
(troubled)
The skinny ghost with the white dog?

BUNNY
Don't say I dreamed it.

Bunny drifts off to sleep.

EXT. OCEAN—BILLY'S SKIFF—DAY

OPEN ON BILLY, *calmly giving instructions:*

BILLY
Good. Good. Now coax her a wee bit to starboard.

REVEAL QUOYLE, *in* MUTE, WHITE-KNUCKLED TERROR,
attempting to pilot the boat.

BILLY *(cont'd)*
But *watch* your starboard.

Quoyle sees a rock off starboard, and adjusts the tiller to avoid it.
Heaves a deep breath: this is harrowing.

BILLY *(cont'd)*
(laughs)
Attaboy. You're a Quoyle. Seawater in your veins.

Quoyle tries to smile, but the terror is still in his eyes.

BILLY *(cont'd)*
How's things with your girl?

QUOYLE
Bunny's still adjusting . . . to things.

BILLY
I was talkin' about Wavey Prowse.

This catches Quoyle off-guard: he loses his focus, inadvertently
swerves the boat, and Billy nearly pitches overboard—

BILLY *(cont'd)*

Whoa! Jesus!

QUOYLE

Sorry. Sorry.
                    (regains control of boat)
We're just friends, me and Wavey.

BILLY

Fine. You don't have to drown me over it.

EXT. GAZE ISLAND—DAY

as BILLY *and* QUOYLE *drag the skiff onto the shore.*

QUOYLE

Were you ever married, Billy?

*Billy doesn't answer right away. He secures the skiff. He motions
for Quoyle to follow him up toward a hillside path:*

BILLY

This way.

As they walk together:

BILLY *(cont'd)*
(hesitantly)
Between you and me, I had a . . . personal affliction. Half
that stuff, that sex stuff that Nutbeem and Tert Card spews
out, I don't know what they mean.

*They walk together. Quoyle says nothing, just accepts without
judgment what Billy is revealing.*

> BILLY *(cont'd)*
>
> I'm long past wonderin' about it. All I know is, women are
> shaped like leaves, and men fall.

They keep on walking up the steep path.

EXT. A SMALL, WINDY, NEGLECTED CEMETERY—LATER

QUOYLE *and* BILLY *reach the cemetery, which is high up on Gaze Island—the sea spread 360 degrees around them.*

> BILLY
>
> This is where I grew up.
> > *(points to a headstone:)*
> There's me poor father, there.

They walk a bit, and Quoyle notices a grave with the name "QUOYLE."

Billy nods. He points down the weedy slope, to the ancient rusted remains of concrete stairs:

> BILLY *(cont'd)*
>
> That's where your house stood.

Quoyle stares at the spot.

> QUOYLE
>
> Before they dragged it over the ice.

> BILLY
> > *(nods)*
> Before they was driven away.

Quoyle looks up at Billy.

> QUOYLE
>
> Driven away . . . ?

                          BILLY
Aye.
                        (a BEAT)
You didn't know?

Quoyle shakes his head no.

                      BILLY *(cont'd)*
                     (back-peddling)
Ah, well, it ain't neither here nor there. Point is, they made
a new place for theirselves—

                         QUOYLE
                     (cutting him off)
Why, Billy? Why were they driven away?

Billy purses his lips, considering whether to tell Quoyle.

                     QUOYLE *(cont'd)*
It's my blood. Tell it.

After a moment, Billy sighs.

                          BILLY
Well. They come to Gaze Island centuries ago. They was
wrackers. Pirates, sorta like.
                       (pointing)
See them cairns? Fires used to burn in 'em, to guide the
ships at sea. Like lighthouses. Now the Quoyles, they'd
move the fires.

Quoyle looks at Billy in puzzlement.

                     BILLY *(cont'd)*
To fool the ships. Lure 'em into the rocks. So's the Quoyles
could grab the loot.

Quoyle stares at Billy, absorbing it . . .

BILLY *(cont'd)*
They was a savage lot, the old Quoyles.
(a BEAT)
One day they finally went too far. Nailed a man to a tree by his ears, cut off his nose for the scent of blood to draw the nippers and flies that devoured him alive.

Quoyle is sickened.

BILLY *(cont'd)*
Yep. That's when the Quoyles was given their walking papers.

QUOYLE
(barely able to speak)
Jesus . . . Anything else I should know?

BILLY
That about covers it.

CUT TO:

EXT. OCEAN—BILLY'S SKIFF—DAY

QUOYLE *at the tiller once again, doing a little better this time.*

BILLY
You're gettin' the hang of it. You'll be a sea salt 'fore long.

QUOYLE
(suddenly alarmed:)
What's that?

A sudden BANK OF FOG *across the water.*

BILLY
(worried)
Give 'er here.

Billy takes over and the skiff is suddenly IN THE MIDDLE OF THE WHITE FOG. *Quoyle can't see where they are going or how Billy is steering. Quoyle's sees a* HUGE ROCK LOOMING AT THEM *out of the fog, dwarfing the skiff:*

> QUOYLE
> *(terrified)*
>
> Billy!

> BILLY
>
> That's fog loom. Makes a skiff look like an oil tanker.

Quoyle can't breath. As the skiff moves through the fog and rocks like a ghost boat, Billy starts to SING *in a creaking tenor:*

> BILLY *(cont'd)*
>
> "When the Knitting Pins you is abreast, / Pull the tiller to the west."

Quoyle—watching Billy deftly steer through the fog past a SERIES OF SPIKING ROCKS THAT LOOK LIKE PINS—*realizes with amazement that Billy is using the song to navigate past obstacles.*

> BILLY *(cont'd)*
>
> "Behind the pins you must steer / Til the Old Man's Shoe does appear."

Sure enough, they glide past a ROCK FORMATION THAT LOOKS LIKE A SHOE. *Quoyle starts breathing again.*

Billy, skillfully navigating through the fog, gives Quoyle a wink.

But Quoyle still looks troubled . . .

. . . and AS THE SKIFF MOVES THROUGH THE DENSE, DREAMLIKE FOG:

OVERLAP SOUND: *the* MOANING OF THE CABLES *of the Green House in the wind, and . . .*

EXT. THE ISLAND—NIGHT (MANY YEARS AGO)

IMPRESSIONISTIC IMAGES *of mayhem on a ship that has crashed up against the rocks.*

Throats being cut; valuable objects being looted . . .

We still hear the MOANING OF THE CABLES . . .

INTERCUT:

INT. GREEN HOUSE—BEDROOM—NIGHT

ON QUOYLE'S FACE, *almost asleep, but sickened by the* AWFUL SOUND OF THE CABLES *as he lies in bed.*

INTERCUT:

EXT. FROZEN OCEAN—TWILIGHT

The vast world of white. The MASSIVE RUMBLING, *the dogs* BARKING, *the* VOICES *straining with exertion.*

The QUOYLE MEN AND WOMEN *pulling the ropes.*

ROCKS AND STICKS *are being thrown at the Quoyles from behind them. We hear the* ANGRY VOICES OF A MOB *in the distance behind them.*

INTERCUT:

QUOYLE LYING IN BED

Quoyle's face is pale, exhausted, drowsing toward uneasy sleep. The MOANING OF THE CABLES *is loud and plaintive.*

INTERCUT:

EXT. FROZEN OCEAN—TWILIGHT

We now see an ANGRY MOB, SCREAMING EPITHETS, *throwing rocks and sticks at:*

THE QUOYLE MEN AND WOMEN

pulling the house across the ice, away from the mob. One of the women is PETAL. *One of the men is* QUOYLE'S FATHER, *who is yelling with angry disapproval at* YOUNG QUOYLE *(age 8)—who is trying to help pull the house, but he keeps pathetically slipping on the ice.*

And in b.g. we GET A FLEETING GLIMPSE *of a* MAN'S BODY NAILED TO A TREE, *with his* EARS AND NOSE CUT OFF, *and we:*

CUT TO:

INT. BEDROOM IN THE GREEN HOUSE—MORNING

QUOYLE *wakes up, sweat-drenched, from his dream.*

INT. GREEN HOUSE—STAIRS—MORNING

QUOYLE *comes downstairs, and is surprised to find* AGNIS *and* BUNNY *sitting side-by-side on a rug, working together on a necklace—made out of fabric scraps from Agnis's shop.*

QUOYLE

Good morning.

Neither Agnis nor Bunny look up from working on the necklace:

AGNIS
(to Bunny)

See? If you make the loops bigger, you don't have to make as many.

QUOYLE
(*irritated*)
Could I have a word with you, Aunt?

She looks up, and sees that he means business.

INT. KITCHEN—A LITTLE LATER

QUOYLE *facing* AGNIS *across the kitchen table.*

AGNIS
I don't see the problem.

QUOYLE
It's an obsession, these necklaces.

AGNIS
A harmless one.

QUOYLE
(*a* BEAT, *uneasily:*)
Petal always wore necklaces.

Agnis shrugs: so?

Then, out of the blue, Quoyle points to an ANTIQUE CHAIR *over in the corner:*

QUOYLE (*cont'd*)
Where's that chair from?

Agnis is puzzled by Quoyle's non sequitor:

AGNIS
Excuse me?

QUOYLE
That chair. Exotic. Foreign. Not from around here, is it?

Agnis squints at Quoyle: what the hell is he trying to say?

QUOYLE *(cont'd)*
I don't want pirates' loot in this home.

Agnis absorbs this. She studies him a moment.

QUOYLE *(cont'd)*
Billy Pretty told me all about it. Our glorious past.
(pointedly)
It's about time somebody did.

Agnis is not the least bit apologetic:

AGNIS
I don't believe in dwelling on the past.

QUOYLE
No? Then what are we doing here?

AGNIS
Making a future.

This silences Quoyle.

INT. SKIPPER WILL'S DINER—DAY

QUOYLE *and* NUTBEEM *are eating squidburgers. (In b.g. at the
counter, we see master boat-builder* ALVIN YARK, *a slight, fuzzy-
browed oddly elfin old man, holding forth to a group of patrons,
who raptly hang on his every word.)*

Quoyle sees an unwelcome sight: TERT CARD *is heading this way.*

CARD
Well if it ain't the second coming of the Quoyles. Takin' a
long and sumptuous lunch break, I can't help noticing.

*Quoyle swallows a mouthful of squidburger. He tries to ignore
Card, but we can see he's a little rattled.*

CARD *(cont'd)*
(digging at Quoyle)
Sure hope you've got an idea for your next column. Hate
for Jack to think it was beginner's luck, eh?

NUTBEEM
Let the man digest, Tert.

CARD
Mind you, if I was the esteemed author of the shipping news
column—

NUTBEEM
—which mercifully you are not—

CARD
—I'd pick up this McGonigle oil field story. Petrodollars. A
golden flood a jobs. You write about *that*, I'll put it on page
one.

NUTBEEM
("get lost")
Thanks for stopping by, Tert.

QUOYLE
(seconding the motion)
Give our warmest regards to anyone you see.

Tert snarls and flounces off. When he's gone:

NUTBEEM
(re: Card)
He owns Mobil Oil.
(off Quoyle's puzzled look)
Ten shares.

EXT. WAVEY'S YARD—DAY

KIDS, *bundled up against the cold, are playing in the yard.*

QUOYLE *drops off* BUNNY, *gives her a kiss, and turns to go back
to his car.*

WAVEY (O.S.)

Hey.

Quoyle turns, sees WAVEY approaching.

WAVEY *(cont'd)*

Friends usually say hello to friends.

QUOYLE

Oh. Yeah, well, I didn't see you there.

That was lame, and Quoyle knows it.

QUOYLE *(cont'd)*

Look. What happened the other day . . . I'm sorr—

WAVEY

Don't be.

Quoyle studies her, wondering how she means that.

WAVEY *(cont'd)*

I'm making a huge pot of cod chowder tonight. Could use some help eating it.

Quoyle thinks it over . . .

INT. WAVEY'S KITCHEN—EVENING

BUNNY *sits at the little table eating dessert: caramel corn and ice cream. Little* HERRY *is at her side, watching* Freakazoid *on a tiny TV. Bunny shovels in a mouthful of caramel corn. Still chewing, she takes another huge handful of caramel corn . . .*

. . . and Herry opens his mouth like a baby bird, and Bunny stuffs the snack in. It's a stare-and-chew, side by side.

INT. WAVEY'S LIVING ROOM—SAME

QUOYLE *sits in a Barcalounger eating from another bowl of caramel corn, watching a fierce hockey game on a modest TV.*

> QUOYLE
> *(to the TV)*
He high-sticked him!

WAVEY is curled on the sofa, knitting.

> QUOYLE *(cont'd)*
> *(to the TV)*
Oh come *on*, ref, put the sonofabitch in the penalty box!

Wavey's eyes sparkle with amusement. Quoyle sees this.

> QUOYLE *(cont'd)*
What.

> WAVEY
Interesting.

> QUOYLE
What is?

> WAVEY
That little bit of steam in your boiler.

Quoyle doesn't know whether to be proud or embarrassed:

> QUOYLE
Well they shoulda called a penalty.

> WAVEY
> *(slight smile)*
Yeah. I got that.

He returns his gaze to the TV set. But she's not finished with him yet:

> WAVEY *(cont'd)*
What about your column?

He looks up at her again.

WAVEY *(cont'd)*
You said you'd read it to me.

QUOYLE
Oh, yeah well . . .
(a BEAT)
I dunno, maybe after the game . . .

At just this moment, we hear from the TV *a* FINAL BUZZER, *and an* ANNOUNCER *gives the final score.*
Wavey raises an eyebrow: well?

Quoyle reluctantly turns off the TV with the remote, and picks up a TYPEWRITTEN PAGE *from an end table.*

Wavey puts down her book.

Quoyle clears his throat. Oh boy, this is hard for him. Here goes:

QUOYLE *(cont'd)*
"Nobody Hangs a Picture of an Oil Tanker." That's the header.

Wavey keeps looking at him: go on.

QUOYLE *(cont'd)*
"There's a 1904 photo hung in the Killick-Claw library. Eight schooners heading out to the fishing grounds. Their sails are white and beautiful."

The next part means something to him. We hear it in his voice:

QUOYLE *(cont'd)*
"But nowadays, you're just as likely to see the big black shape of an oil tanker. Like the ruptured *Golden Goose*. Last week it leaked 14,000 tones of crude onto seabirds, fish, and boats at Cape Despond."

He sneaks a glance at her, to see what she thinks so far. But all he gets is Wavey's steady, inscrutable gaze.

QUOYLE *(cont'd)*

"There will be more and more tankers. They will get old and corroded, and their tanks will split. And there will be less fish. And less fisherman."
(a pause; the capper:)
"Nobody hangs a picture of an oil tanker on their wall."

Silence. He looks up.

QUOYLE *(cont'd)*

Well? What do you think?

She considers. Then:

WAVEY

I think when Tert Card sees it, he'll sit up nights thinking of cheap shots to pay you back. I think he'll never stop until you're fired.

Quoyle swallows. She's probably right.

WAVEY *(cont'd)*

I think I haven't been so proud of a friend . . . since I don't know when.

Quoyle's eyes shine. There is a long silence.

QUOYLE

Did I tell you how much I like homemade caramel corn?

She nods. He stuffs a handful of caramel corn into his mouth.

EXT. THE GREEN HOUSE—NIGHT

It's a FOGGY night. BUNNY jumps out of the station wagon, runs to the house. As QUOYLE locks his car:

BUNNY (O.S.)

The Skinny Ghost must be here.

He looks up. The front door is OPEN.

> BUNNY *(cont'd)*
> Can I keep the necklace?

Inside the doorway is a long piece of TWINE. *There are* KNOTS *neatly tied along its length. Quoyle stares, frightened.*

> BUNNY *(cont'd)*
> Do you think he's in the house?

> QUOYLE
> *(trying to sound calm)*
> Sweetie. Come sit in the car.

INT. FRONT HALLWAY—NIGHT

Quoyle climbing the stairs in fading light, carrying a tire iron. He stops midway; listens to the silence.

> QUOYLE
> If anybody's there, come out now!

Up, up, to the top. He looks down the empty hall and sees:

KNOTTED TWINE . . . *at every door.*

Quoyle is spooked. Then, he happens to glance through a window:

QUOYLE'S P.O.V. (THROUGH WINDOW)

Indistinct images: Are they just SHADOWS *roiling in the fog—or are they an* IMPOSSIBLY SKINNY MAN *and a* WHITE DOG *running away from the house?*

> QUOYLE *(cont'd)*
> Hey! Hey!!!

But the ambiguous images DISAPPEAR *into the* FOG.

QUOYLE *is disconcerted.*

Now AGNIS, *groggy, sticks her head out of a bedroom. It's obvious Quoyle has awakened her from sleep; she stares irritably at him.*

                          QUOYLE
     I think I just saw . . . something . . . out there . . .

Agnis is unimpressed.

                          AGNIS
     The fog. It plays tricks.

                          QUOYLE
     Well, but—
                              (re: twine)
     I found—

                          AGNIS

(heading back into her room; sharply:)
     Good night. And please keep your voice down.

She forcefully shuts the door. Quoyle blinks.

INT. GAMMY BIRD—MORNING

QUOYLE *enters, tired and distracted. The place is lit, but empty. A toilet* FLUSHES, *and* CARD *emerges from the loo.*

                          CARD
     So tell me. You fancy it?

Card nods toward something behind Quoyle. Quoyle turns and sees, hanging over Card's desk: a large framed PHOTO *of "QUIET EYE—WORLD'S LARGEST OIL TANKER." Quoyle stares blankly.*

                          QUOYLE
     Like I said. Nobody hangs those.

Card just goes to the fresh stack of newspapers on his desk, and hands one to Quoyle:

> CARD
>
> Your column's front page stuff. Only now, it's more like a caption, is all.

On the front page is the same PHOTO *of the tanker that's on Card's wall.*

> QUOYLE
> *(reads)*
> "More than 3000 tankers proudly ride the world's seas. Even the biggest take advantage of Newfoundland's deepwater ports and refineries."

> CARD
>
> Spelled everthin' perfect. So as not t'embarrass ya.

> QUOYLE
> *(reading)*
> "Oil and Newfoundland go together like ham and eggs, and like ham and eggs they'll nourish us in the coming years."

> CARD
>
> Even put your name on it.

> QUOYLE
> *(finishes reading)*
> "Let's all hang a picture of an oil tanker on our wall."

Quoyle stares in disbelief at the newspaper in his hand.

> CARD
>
> Man a your principles. I understand resignation is the only honorable course.

Quoyle, seething, drops the paper on the floor . . . and steps on it, on his way to the door.

> CARD (*cont'd*)
> If you're off to see Jack Buggit, you'll have to swim.

Quoyle turns back.

> CARD (*cont'd*)
> You can whine and beg him. But I runs his paper, every inch
> of it, every dirty time-eatin' job which *he* would have t'do
> without me.
> > (*a wink*)
> An' if you think he's gonna choose *you* over fishing . . .
> you're dumber than you look, if that's possible.

Quoyle storms out, SLAMS *the door. Card smiles.*

EXT. KILLICK-CLAW DOCK—DAY

QUOYLE *approaches his boat. A few old* FISHERMAN *are
nearby; some of them glance at Quoyle with mild, deadpan
amusement.*

*Quoyle eyes his boat apprehensively, as if facing an adversary.
Then, nervous but determined, he gets into the boat and launches
it . . .*

> > > > **CUT TO:**

EXT. THE BAY—JACK IN HIS FISHING BOAT—DAY

JACK *is fishing . . . when he sees a* LITTLE BOAT *coming toward
him: it's* QUOYLE, *scared as hell, unsteadily piloting his "shit
boat."*

> QUOYLE
> > (*nervous; trying to sound "authentic":*)
> Ahoy, Jack!

*Jack, amused, watches Quoyle's hapless struggle to pull his own
boat up alongside Jack's.*

JACK
(shakes his head)
Oh for chrissake, Quoyle, just cut your cockadoodle engine!
I'll come to you.

Quoyle, embarrassed, cuts his engine. Jack pulls alongside him.

JACK *(cont'd)*
Now, what's the emergency? Can't it wait till I'm done
fishin'?

Quoyle clears his throat. Tries to work up his nerve.

QUOYLE
It's about my column.

JACK
That can wait.

Jack starts to turn back to his fishing apparatus, until:

QUOYLE
(blurting)
Card didn't print it how I wrote it.

JACK
(irritably)
So?

Quoyle doesn't know what else to say.

JACK *(cont'd)*
You disapprove how Card runs my newspaper?

After a moment, Quoyle nervously nods his head yes.

JACK *(cont'd)*
(cold, hard)
Enough to lose your job?

Quoyle blinks a few times.

> QUOYLE
>
> I . . .

> JACK
>
> Yes or no.

Then:

> QUOYLE
> *(quiet, his voice cracking)*
>
> Yes.

Jack gives him a hard glare. Quoyle gulps.

INT. GAMMY BIRD—DAY

QUOYLE *is pensively chomping on a donut from a boxful of donuts on the desk.* NUTBEEM, *leaning against Quoyle's desk, is also eating a donut, and* BILLY *is bringing over three mugs of coffee. They seem to be awaiting a verdict.*

Through the glass of the only private office . . .

. . . JACK BUGGIT *is talking to* CARD. *Card stands now, strides to the door, flings it* OPEN. *Nutbeem taps Quoyle's shoulder. They look to Card.*

> CARD
>
> So. This is what Jack and I think.

Card is seething, but trying to seem defiant, looking Quoyle straight in the eye.

> CARD *(cont'd)*
>
> We wanna run Quoyle's wrong-headed oil spill piece 'cause controversy sells papers and papers sells ads.

Quoyle is surprised . . . Through the window to Jack's office, he sees the slightest trace of a smile on Jack's face.

CARD *(cont'd)*
(defiant; keeping his laser gaze on Quoyle)
But the oil tanker picture *stays*!

Nutbeem's eyes widen; he mimes catching an arrow shot through his chest, and falls OFF *the desk.*

EXT. STREET OUTSIDE SKIPPER WILL'S DINER—EVENING

WAVEY *and* QUOYLE *get out of Quoyle's station wagon. Quoyle has a little bit of a strut in his walk tonight.*

QUOYLE
It was a beautiful moment. I wish you could've seen Tert's face.

WAVEY
("no thanks")
That's alright, I've seen it.

Quoyle laughs, a little too much; he's rather giddy with today's triumph.

INT. SKIPPER WILL'S DINER—EVENING

QUOYLE *and* WAVEY *enter together.*

The CASHIER *and a* WAITRESS *are eyeing* QUOYLE *with interest, wondering if he and Wavey are an item.*

Quoyle and Wavey see a table where DENNIS, NUTBEEM, *and* BILLY *are sitting, enjoying squidburgers and beer. They nod hello.*

Quoyle and Wavey pick up menus from the cash register counter. They take a look at their menus . . .

. . . but then Quoyle and Wavey can't help noticing Dennis,

114

Nutbeem, Billy, and VARIOUS PATRONS *of the diner sneaking furtive, intrigued glances their way.*

> WAVEY
> *(to Quoyle)*
> How would you feel about ordering "to go"?

EXT. THE HARBOR—NIGHT

WAVEY *and* QUOYLE *sit huddled together on a piling as they eat dinner from "to-go" cartons. It looks like a parody of a romantic picnic: they're shivering from the cold, their hands trembling as they eat. A half-consumed six-pack of beer is at their feet; they're both slightly tipsy and GIGGLING.*

Quoyle opens another carton of food. He looks at it's contents with puzzlement and foreboding.

> WAVEY

Seal Flipper Pie.

> QUOYLE
> *(clueless)*

Of course.

> WAVEY

It's not the flipper actually. It's the slimy, knuckly, cartilidge part.

> QUOYLE
> *(a BEAT; an excuse;)*

I'm uh . . . Pretty full, actually. Had a big lunch.

He pats his tummy to dramatize his fullness. But Wavey is not letting him off the hook:

> WAVEY

They say you're not really a Newfoundlander till you've eaten seal-flipper pie.

Quoyle gulps.

> QUOYLE
> Is that what they say?

Wavey nods: damn right.

Quoyle steels himself. Takes a big bite. Chews. It's rough going. Another bite. Wavey is watching him closely, trying not to laugh.

> QUOYLE
> *(mouth full)*
> Wow. Good. Mm. Christ.

He manfully swallows it. She bursts out laughing:

> WAVEY
> Never eat it myself.

> QUOYLE
> You don't?

She's laughing hard. He starts laughing too. She takes out another container of food:

> WAVEY
> *(through her laughter)*
> Here's some real food.

EXT. OMALOOR BAY—QUOYLE'S "SHIT BOAT"—DAY

QUOYLE *is at the rudder of his ungainly boat. He's still nervous in the water—but this time, we also detect a glint of celebration, of triumph, in his eyes . . . maybe a shred of confidence.*

He goes around a point, and something catches his eye:

A MAN'S BODY *in a yellow suit. Arms and legs spread out like a starfish, the body slides in and out of a small cave. The body has* NO HEAD.

Quoyle stares in frozen shock.

Then Quoyle WHEELS *the boat around.* KICKS *it in overdrive toward the town across the bay.*

Clear of the point, panic-ridden Quoyle is going much faster than he should—

—and when he tries to adjust the tiller, he loses control—and the BOAT FLIPS OVER—

—and Quoyle goes FLYING INTO THE WATER, *limbs flailing in all directions . . .*

INTERCUT:

QUOYLE'S FATHER FLINGING *him into the water;* YOUNG QUOYLE SINKING *like an anvil in a profusion of bubbles, and* CUT . . .

BACK TO QUOYLE

underwater, struggling madly somehow to the surface, thrashing toward the overturned boat. He grasps the stilled propeller blade, which CUTS HIS HAND—*but he still holds on, which causes the bow to lift; the next wave turns the boat upright, filling it with water, and it* SINKS *forever.*

Quoyle TUMBLES *once more beneath the surface, watching the boat* DISAPPEAR *into darkness below him.*

Once more Quoyle THRASHES UP, GASPING, TO THE SURFACE . . .

And he sees:

PETAL

daintily rowing a small boat, unaffected by the waves, her filmy dress rippling in light breeze.

Is her lilting smile cruel? Or is it only the sort of irony that conveys intimacy, even affection?

AND SHE VANISHES. IN HER PLACE, BOBS A RED PLASTIC COOLER. HE LUNGES FOR IT, GRIPS THE HANDLE—AND MANAGES TO STAY AFLOAT ATOP THE COOLER.

QUOYLE, *far from shore, rises and falls with the sea swells.*

CUT TO:

HOURS LATER—QUOYLE,

barely conscious, still clings somehow to the Red Cooler. The light in the sky is fading.

And then he sees a distant BEAM OF LIGHT, *approaching.* A FISHING BOAT.

The BEAM OF LIGHT *draws close to him. He can see the silhouette of a man in the boat.*

The boat pulls up alongside Quoyle. He squints his swollen eyes, as STRONG HANDS PULL HIM UP *from the Red Cooler, out of the water.*

A voice warbles, DISTORTED BY WIND AND QUOYLE'S DIMINISHED CONSCIOUSNESS:

> JACK
> Jesus Cockadoodle Christ! I *knowed* somebody was out here.

Quoyle's teeth are chattering hard, his body shivering painfully;

JACK *hauls him over the rail and lays him down on a wriggling mound of fish.*

Quoyle burrows into the fish, like nestling in a down comforter. Jack covers him with a heavy tarp.

Then Jack lifts the RED COOLER *into his boat. He yanks it open—*

—and out rolls a HUMAN HEAD *with a great mass of white hair: the head of* BAYONET MELVILLE, *which comes to rest only inches from Quoyle's own shivering face. Quoyle* GASPS *through his chattering teeth, staring into Melville's great, swollen, lifeless face.*

INT. JACK BUGGIT'S ATTIC—NIGHT

QUOYLE *lies in bed, feverish and asleep, his body made larger by mounds of bedclothes, topped by a crocheted rug. His left hand is* BANDAGED.

He stirs awake to see: Jack's wife EDNA BUGGIT *in the doorway, leading* WAVEY *into the room.*

> EDNA
> *(whisper to Wavey)*
> He's still burning off the fever.

Wavey sits down at Quoyle's bedside. He weakly looks up at her.

Out in the hallway, BILLY, NUTBEEM, *and* JACK *cluster by the door, peering into the room.*

> BILLY
> *(to Quoyle)*
> We'll need a quote, boy.

> JACK
> Something for the front page—

                         WAVEY
                  (sharply cutting them off)
         You guys are worse than my preschoolers.

The guys all fall silent. Edna heads for the door:

                         EDNA
                  (quiet, firm, to the guys)
              Go on, shoo. He needs rest.

*Jack, Billy, and Nutbeem exchange chastened glances as Edna herds
them away.*

*Wavey, alone now with Quoyle, studies him with concern. With
nurselike precision, she reaches under the covers and touches his
toes:*

                         WAVEY
              Any feeling yet?

                        QUOYLE
              Tingles a little.

                         WAVEY
              You're lucky.

                        QUOYLE
                       (weakly)
              I'm fine. I'll be ready to get back in the water in twenty,
              thirty years.

But she doesn't laugh. She almost looks a little angry.

Quoyle looks at her questioningly.

                         WAVEY
              Do you know how close you were to dead?

Quoyle nods.

WAVEY *(cont'd)*
Get my uncle Alvin Yark to build you a proper boat. And learn how to use it. Any questions?

Quoyle shakes his head no.

WAVEY *(cont'd)*
Good.

She leans down and gently kisses his forehead. Quoyle inhales the scent of her.

She stands up and walks out of the room with her cool grace. Quoyle, his eyes tired and watery, just watches her go.

INT. AGNIS'S SHOP—DAY

OPEN CLOSE *on a worktable, on which rests the* GAMMY BIRD *with a* HUGE BANNER HEADLINE:

MURDERED MILLIONAIRE FOUND IN BAY!
Gammy Bird Reporter Scoops National Press

WIDEN *to include* AGNIS *and* MAVIS *are both hard at work sewing upholstery.*

MAVIS
(fascinated)
Were the eyes open or closed?

AGNIS
Don't know. He just said it was a disembodied head.

MAVIS
What did the police have to say about it?

AGNIS
They're workin' on it.
(shrugs)
Little late to return the head to its owner, though.

Mavis's eyes widen, and she laughs: you're terrible.

The door opens, and QUOYLE *hurries in excitedly with a Police Bulletin in his hand.*

>   MAVIS
> Well if it isn't the famed journalist himself.

>   QUOYLE
>   Police Bulletin:
>   *(reads)*
> "Mrs. Silver Melville was arrested early today in Lanai,
> Hawaii, for the murder of her husband, socialite and
> raconteur Mr. Bayonet Melville. "He pushed me once too
> often," Mrs. Melville confessed, "so I finally pushed back."

>   AGNIS
>   *(impulsively, almost fiercely)*
> *Good for you, lady.*

Quoyle and Mavis are both taken aback by Agnis's reaction.

Agnis sees the way they're both looking at her.

>   AGNIS *(cont'd)*
>   *(unapologetic)*
> Well, he prob'ly deserved it.

EXT. ALVIN YARK'S WORK SHED—DAY

OPEN ON *a half-built little boat up on trestles.* ALVIN YARK, *the old master, is patiently building the boat.*

>   ALVIN
>   (SINGING *while he works:)*
> "Oh the Gandy Goose, she ain't no use,/'Cause all her
> nuts'n bolts is loose."

BILLY *leads* QUOYLE *into the work area.*

Alvin glances up and sees them—but continues working on the boat. Quoyle is confused.

Quoyle starts to speak—but Billy instantly SHUSHES *him: one doesn't interrupt Alvin Yark while he's at work.*

Quoyle watches Alvin working and humming the "Gandy Goose" song. Finally Alvin looks up from his work.

The old man approaches Quoyle, looks him over, taking the measure of the man. This makes Quoyle uneasy.

> ALVIN *(cont'd)*
> Fifteen footer'll do you. Outboard rodney. Put a little seven 'orsepower motor on 'er.
> *(nods to himself, satisfied with his diagnosis)*
> Have somethin' for you by springtime. If I gets out in the woods and finds just the right timber. See, you must find good uns, your stem, you wants to bring it down with a bit of a 'ollow to it—

> QUOYLE
> I thought you'd have materials on hand.

Alvin looks surprised, almost amused. Billy closes his eyes in embarrassment at Quoyle's glaring ignorance.

> ALVIN
> No, boy, I doesn't build with dry wood. The boat takes up the water if 'ers made with dry wood.

Alvin turns away, brings up phlegm and hawks it into a pile of sawdust. He resumes working in the half-built boat.

Billy starts to lead Quoyle out—but then:

> ALVIN *(cont'd)*
> *(while he works; not looking up)*
> Quoyle, How's Wavey Prowse?

QUOYLE
(a BEAT)
Why you asking *me*?

Alvin works and sings a bit more. Then:

ALVIN
Is it the boy, then?

Quoyle doesn't understand.

ALVIN *(cont'd)*
Stoppin' you two gettin' together?

QUOYLE
No. Herry's a good kid. It's not . . .
(a sigh)
I'm sure you know about her husband's accident . . .

BILLY
Alvin's the one found Herold's boat.

Alvin hawks some more phlegm into the sawdust.

ALVIN
Odd, how 'er hull was cracked from the inside. Don't often
see that.

QUOYLE
Why not?

Alvin doesn't answer, just keeps working on the boat.

ALVIN
(SINGING)
"Oh the Gandy Goose, she ain't no use,/'Cause all her
nuts'n bolts is loose."

Class dismissed. Billy leads Quoyle out of the workshop.

INT. THE GREEN HOUSE—KITCHEN—NIGHT

QUOYLE *is frying up leftovers (working one-handed, because his left hand is bandaged).*

We hear (o.s.) BUNNY *and* HERRY *clomping around upstairs, playing.*

> QUOYLE
> *(re: his cooking)*
> Don't get your hopes up.

> WAVEY
> *(shrugs)*
> First man who's ever cooked for me. You get a lot of leeway.

BUNNY *and* HERRY *come tearing through the kitchen. Herry has one of Bunny's necklaces, and Bunny is chasing after him to try and retrieve it.*

> BUNNY
> *(upset, screaming at Herry)*
> Give it back!

> WAVEY
> *(sharply)*
> Herry.

But now Bunny TRIPS *and falls, bumping her knee.*

> BUNNY
> *(starts to cry)*
> Oww!

Herry, startled by the trouble he's caused, immediately hands the necklace to Wavey—but before Wavey has a chance to give Bunny the necklace, Bunny angrily grabs it:

> BUNNY *(cont'd)*
> It's not for you!

WAVEY

    I know that.

Wavey gently hugs crying Bunny. Bunny doesn't return the embrace . . . but she also doesn't push Wavey away. Wavey strokes Bunny's hair, quieting her down.

Quoyle intently watches Wavey holding Bunny, calming her, softly murmuring soothing words into her ear.

Wavey looks up and sees Quoyle watching her.

                                      CUT TO:

INT. KITCHEN—LATER

QUOYLE *is nursing a beer while he finishes wiping down the kitchen counters.*

ANGLE-HALLWAY OUTSIDE KITCHEN

WAVEY *comes down the stairs. She's about to enter the kitchen, but just stands there a moment, watching Quoyle, unseen by him.*

Quoyle picks up a framed PHOTO *of Bunny on the countertop, and carefully dusts off the glass covering the photo, then gently sets it down again.*

This tender gesture makes Wavey smile slightly to herself: this man is growing on her.

Quoyle looks up, sees Wavey looking at him.

QUOYLE

    Hey.

WAVEY

    Hey.

She enters the kitchen.

WAVEY *(cont'd)*
Both asleep. In Bunny's bed.

QUOYLE
Do we trust them?

Wavey laughs gently. She stands next to him at the counter.

QUOYLE *(cont'd)*
(offers his beer)
Want a sip?

WAVEY
Yeah. I do.

She takes his beer:

WAVEY *(cont'd)*
To your health.

It's the same thing Petal once said to him—and for a split-second he sees PETAL *swigging the beer; a visual echo of the much-earlier moment back in the old house in Mockingburg . . .*

. . . and instantly it's WAVEY *again.*

Wavey takes his bandaged hand in her own. She feels happy, relaxed. Comfortable with him. She lightly, playfully drums her fingers against his bandaged palm.

WAVEY *(cont'd)*
Can you feel that through your bandage?

He nods.

She looks into his eyes. She slowly leans in to kiss him . . . but then senses that something is wrong.

WAVEY *(cont'd)*

What?

Quoyle doesn't know what to say. Then:

QUOYLE

So he never cooked a meal? Your husband.

Wavey looks at him with puzzlement, and maybe a trace of anger.

WAVEY

Why are we talking about my husband?

QUOYLE

Because I understand. You said it's four years ago, and it's yesterday. I understand that.

Wavey slides the beer can away from her.

WAVEY

My husband isn't who we're talking about. Right?

Quoyle says nothing. He can't meet Wavey's steady gaze. He just sits there, trapped by the pathetic truth about himself.

WAVEY *(cont'd)*
(with quiet dignity)

I'll go get Herry.
(a BEAT)
He wouldn't like waking up in a strange bed.

She heads out of the kitchen and goes upstairs.

Quoyle, alone in the kitchen, shakes his head:

QUOYLE
(to himself)

"Miserable Man Wrecks Friendship."

INT. SKIPPER WILL'S DINER—DAY

QUOYLE *sits alone at a table, gazing forlornly out the window. He has a squidburger in front of him, but he hasn't touched it. The bandage is no longer on his hand; Quoyle is glumly flexing and unflexing his hand.*

NUTBEEM *and* BILLY, *laughing about something, come over to the table and sit down with Quoyle.*

Nutbeem, seeing that Quoyle's in a funk, jabs him with an elbow:

> NUTBEEM
> How's the house coming along, mate?

Quoyle shrugs.

> QUOYLE
> *(without energy)*
> Got it fixed up pretty good . . . but now Aunt tells me we gotta move. For the winter.

Billy and Nutbeem look at him questioningly.

> QUOYLE *(cont'd)*
> Three hours to drive here from the Point. All the ice. Alvin Yark won't have my boat ready for another couple months.
> *(sighs)*
> Agnis can stay over her shop. Bunny and me have to find a room in town.

Billy studies Quoyle a moment. Then:

> BILLY
> How's Wavey?

> QUOYLE
> I *told* you: we're *friends.*

Billy holds up his hands: sorry I asked.

NUTBEEM

If it's a place to stay you need, you can take my trailer.
Timing's perfect.

Quoyle looks at Nutbeem:

QUOYLE

What do you mean?

BILLY

He means he's leaving us, the rootless traitor.

NUTBEEM

My boat's ready. If I stay any longer, I may begin to like it
here.

Quoyle is quite surprised.

NUTBEEM *(cont'd)*

I'm throwing myself a farewell party on Saturday.
Departure to follow Sunday. Regrets, soon after, no doubt.

Quoyle absorbs this. He'll be sorry to lose Nutbeem.

INT. GREEN HOUSE—BEDROOM—NIGHT

QUOYLE *lies in bed, awake, restless, unable to sleep.* BUNNY *is
asleep, clutching his shirt for security.*

Then Quoyle HEARS *something else outside: a* DOG BARKING,
and an OLD MAN'S VOICE *shushing the dog.*

Quoyle gets up, goes to the window, peers down through the FOG,
and SEES:

THE SKINNY OLD MAN AND THE WHITE DOG *stealing
through the fog toward the house. The Skinny Old Man takes several
pieces of* KNOTTED TWINE *from his ratty pocket. He starts to
place one twine at the front door, when suddenly:*

QUOYLE yells at him:

QUOYLE

Hey!

THE SKINNY OLD MAN *looks up in alarm, and runs away.*

QUOYLE *hurriedly pulls on a parka and races downstairs, and:*

(EXT.) A JAGGED, FAST-PACED SERIES OF SHOTS (NIGHT)

Quoyle racing out of the house with a BROOMSTICK *in hand—*

—and then Quoyle spotting the SKINNY OLD MAN *and the* DOG *racing away through the fog—*

—and Quoyle pursuing them across the point—

—and Quoyle losing sight of them—

—and Quoyle running through the fog—and catching another glimpse of the Skinny Old Man and the Dog

—and Quoyle chasing them across a rocky landscape—and following them down to:

EXT. A DARK COVE—NIGHT

where the Skinny Old Man and the Dog race into a LITTLE HUT *(which is semi-obscured by an overgrown tangle of wild shrubs).*

QUOYLE *runs over to the hut and shoves the door open, and:*

INT. THE HUT—NIGHT

as QUOYLE *bursts in and the Skinny Old Man* SHOUTS, *and the dog* GROWLS VICIOUSLY *and goes for Quoyle's leg. Quoyle fends off the dog with the broomstick.*

                    SKINNY OLD MAN
                        (to dog)
          Down, Floyd!

The dog desists.

The hut is a crazed mess: loops of fishing line underfoot, a churn of splinters, bits of wool, gnawed sheep ribs, fish scales and bones, bark and blood.

The Skinny Old Man suddenly throws the KNOTTED TWINES *into the* BURNING STOVE, *searing them.*

                    SKINNY OLD MAN *(cont'd)*
          Them knots is fixed by fire now!
                        (a threat)
          Now the curse'll never undo!

The Skinny Old Man seals his threat with a piercing CACKLE.

                    SKINNY OLD MAN *(cont'd)*
          You got no business up there in the Quoyle house.

                        QUOYLE
          I am a Quoyle.

                    SKINNY OLD MAN
          I was a Quoyle before you was anything.

Quoyle studies the Skinny Old Man

                    SKINNY OLD MAN *(cont'd)*
          She mighta come visit me. Cousin Agnis.

The Skinny Old Man gives Quoyle a menacing, knowing, brown-toothed grin.

                    SKINNY OLD MAN *(cont'd)*
                        (a perverse wink:)
          Tell 'er hello from Cousin Nolan.

SKINNY OLD MAN *(cont'd)*

She mighta come, only she can't face me. 'Cause I knows what she done.

> *(another wink:)*

She killed him.

A moment of stunned silence. Dare Quoyle ask?

SKINNY OLD MAN *(cont'd)*

The baby she was carryin'. What was she t'do? She was only twelve. It was her own brother that done 'er.

QUOYLE

Her . . . brother . . .

Quoyle is wide-eyed with shock.

OVERLAP *the horrible, insistent* MOANING OF THE CABLES *. . . and* CUT TO:

INT. BEDROOM IN THE GREEN HOUSE—NIGHT

QUOYLE *lying awake in bed, awake, upset. The cables outside* MOANING AND MOANING, *and:*

INTERCUT:

EXT. A TINY FROZEN POND—DAY (LONG AGO)

AGNIS AT *12—just as we saw her in the photo—is skating alone.*

SKINNY OLD MAN (V.O.)

Her brother. She only had the one.

Agnis looks up and sees:

GUY QUOYLE *at 15 (Quoyle's father, whom we also saw in the photo). He steps onto the ice, unbuttons his pants.*

He begins to slide towards her on the soles of his fishing boots. She looks around. Snow banked on all sides of the pond. Nowhere to run on her skates.

SKINNY OLD MAN (V.O.) *(cont'd)*

'Course, no one alive knows no more. 'Cept me.

CUT BACK TO: QUOYLE IN BED

His eyes sparkling with tears.

INTERCUT:

EXT. THE FROZEN POND—DAY

Young Agnis, breathless, skating this way and that. The boy closing in, cutting off her angle. A deadly endgame. He is closing in. And as he grabs her in SLOW-MOTION *and pulls her to the ground . . .*

The o.s. MOANING OF THE CABLES *goes on and on . . .*

CUT TO:

EXT. THE GREEN HOUSE—DAWN

QUOYLE *sits alone on a rock, bundled in his parka, sipping a mug of tea. He clearly hasn't slept much. He gazes uneasily out at the sea.*

Then BUNNY *emerges from the house, shivering in a bathrobe, and runs over to Quoyle:*

BUNNY
(indignant)

I woke up and you weren't there.

QUOYLE

Sorry. Want breakfast?

Bunny doesn't answer him because a nearby object has caught her eye. She takes a few steps and picks up the object: it's a DEAD BIRD, *perfect except for a lolling head.*

> QUOYLE *(cont'd)*
> Put it down, sweetheart. It has germs.

> BUNNY
> Why?

> QUOYLE
> Because it's dead. Broken neck.

Bunny pulls a little wad of Kleenex from her bathrobe pocket and carefully WRAPS THE BIRD *in it, as if in a burial shroud. She gently places the shrouded bird in a little* CREVICE *between two rocks for safekeeping.*

She crouches over it, watching it. No movement. Bunny shivers.

> QUOYLE *(cont'd)*
> Let's go in. You wash your hands, and I'll scramble some eggs.

Quoyle puts his arm around Bunny and leads back toward the house. She hesitates a moment, looks back over her shoulder at the bird interred in the crevice.

> QUOYLE *(cont'd)*
> Come on, sweetheart.

They head into the house.

EXT. NUTBEEM'S TRAILER—NIGHT

The shabby little trailer is overflowing with DRUNKEN MEN, *having a loud party,* MUSIC BLASTING.

INT. NUTBEEM'S TRAILER—SAME

The place is jammed with MEN. *Bottles are passed from hand to hand overhead. A few Men urinate into a barrel of remaining potato chips.*

QUOYLE *is jammed up against the wall, having a drunken,* SHOUTED CONVERSATION *with* NUTBEEM:

> QUOYLE
> My wife is dead!

> NUTBEEM
> I know!

> QUOYLE
> Killed in a car accident! And what does Jack Buggit give me to write? Car wrecks, among other things.

> NUTBEEM
> And what does he give me? I'm to listen to the radio all the day! Me, Nutbeem—the bloke who at age nine learned about his parents' death when he heard it on the fucking BBC! And what does he give Billy the Bachelor?

> QUOYLE
> The bloody Home Page. Bake-offs and baby booties.

> NUTBEEM
> He does know things about people. He's sensitive, alright.
> *(a smile and a shudder)*
> Making us all face our worst fears, eh?

DENNIS *drunkenly squeezes next to Quoyle:*

> DENNIS
> Quoyle of the North!

Quoyle raises his beer bottle in salute.

DENNIS *(cont'd)*
Have you and Wavey done the dirty yet?

Quoyle recoils a bit at the question.

QUOYLE
She's a grieving widow.

DENNIS
Pfff! Grieving for Herold Prowse. That's a good one.

Quoyle looks questioningly at Dennis.

DENNIS *(cont'd)*
Let me tell you somethin' about ol' Herold Prowse! It was like a parlor game in town, to squint at babies and see if they looked like Herold.

This unsettles Quoyle. He guzzles a big swig of beer.

EXT. NUTBEEM'S TRAILER—NIGHT

The party pours out of Nutbeem's trailer, lifted half-off its cinder blocks. A naked man dances in the mud. A truck rams another truck, splintering glass.

QUOYLE *is among the anarchic crowd.*

QUOYLE
Here's to Nutbeem!

Everyone CHEERS *and raises their bottles. A* BIG UGLY GUY *leaps onto a tree stump, brandishing an* AXE.

BIG UGLY GUY
WE ALL LOVES OLD FOOKIN' NUTBEEM, YAR?

Cries of YAR! *fill the woods. Nutbeem himself is* HOISTED *on shoulders, whooping and sloshing his grog.*

BIG UGLY GUY (cont'd)
SO LET'S US *KEEP* 'IM 'ERE! GOT YER CHAIN SAW,
NEDDIE?

An idea that wins IMMEDIATE MASS APPROVAL. *Nutbeem's
eyes open bug-wide, and his shouted protests are drowned out by
the raucous mob, as the Big Ugly Guy leaps onto the deck of*
NUTBEAM'S BOAT *and flicks on a* CHAIN SAW. *An approving
roar from the other men as they join in the destruction. Nutbeem is
half-laughing, half-crying . . .*

A SERIES OF IMPRESSIONISTIC SHOTS

as the anarchic mob WREAKS DESTRUCTION ON NUTBEEM'S
BOAT AND TRAILER—*wielding axes, two-by-fours, pocket-
knives, rocks—anything and everything they can get their hands
on—smashing the boat and trailer with the frenzied camaraderie of
primitive hunters killing an animal.*

QUOYLE *finds himself swept into the spirit of mayhem. He picks up
a 2-by-4 and starts* SMASHING IT INTO THE BOAT *again and
again. It's as if he's releasing all the pent-up frustration of a
lifetime. He's howling and screaming like a wild man . . .*

INTERCUT:

The OLD QUOYLES FIERCELY LOOTING A SHIPWRECK *on*
GAZE ISLAND. *Our modern-day* QUOYLE *is among his
ancestors—and he's as furious and brutal as any of them, looting
and pillaging and screaming with wild-eyed abandon.*

He glances over and sees that PETAL *and* QUOYLE'S FATHER
are also among the looters . . .

BACK TO SCENE

QUOYLE, *running out of energy, growing sickened by his own
violence, stumbles his way out of the rampaging mob.*

He runs off into the woods . . .

EXT. WAVEY'S HOUSE—NIGHT

QUOYLE, *out of breath, sweat-soaked, is on his knees outside a lit window. There is the sound of* ACCORDION MUSIC *from inside.*

Through the window, Quoyle is watching:

WAVEY, *sitting on a stool in her warm kitchen, her skirt wide between her legs as she* PLAYS THE ACCORDION *for grinning Herry to do a jig. Quoyle watches the jigging boy. And Quoyle sees Wavey's concentration and pleasure as she plays the music for her son.*

Quoyle yearns to be part of this . . . but is also tormented and afraid.

INT. WAVEY'S KITCHEN—SAME

Wavey plays with feeling, watching her son's earnest, joyful dance. Suddenly she's startled by a FURIOUS POUNDING ON THE WINDOW.

Alarmed, Wavey stops playing, looks up and sees: QUOYLE AT THE WINDOW—*drunk, disheveled, cold breath steaming from his nostrils—pounding ferociously on the window.*

EXT. WAVEY'S HOUSE—SAME

Wavey opens the back door. Quoyle stares at her; his eyes frightened and dangerous, like a wild animal who's been trapped.

> WAVEY
> What's wrong?

Quoyle's face is flushed, his breathing rapid.

> QUOYLE
> A Quoyle I'm one of the Quoyles. Pirates. Looters. Murderers.

She just stares at him.

> QUOYLE *(cont'd)*
> My father raped his little sister. Oh, and he tried to teach me
> to swim.

His weirdness is beginning to frighten her.

Quoyle impulsively lurches toward her, hugs her tightly.

> WAVEY
> Stop that.

But he only hugs her tighter.

> WAVEY *(cont'd)*
> Jesus. You smell like a brewery.

*Quoyle doesn't let go of her. He nuzzles his face in her neck. His
hands reach for her ass—*

> WAVEY *(cont'd)*
> Stop it!

—she angrily shoves him away, SLAMMING HIM *against the
wall—but he's so drunk he doesn't even feel the pain.*

Herry steps out of the kitchen, stands in the hallway watching them.

> WAVEY *(cont'd)*
> *(firmly, to Herry)*
> Go back in the kitchen, sweetie.

But Herry doesn't go. He just smiles innocently at Quoyle . . .

*. . . and Quoyle smiles back. But Quoyle's smile is tinged with
shame.*

QUOYLE
(to Herry)
I'm sorry.

Herry, a little spooked, goes back into the kitchen.

QUOYLE *(cont'd)*
(to Wavey; barely audible)
I'm sorry, Petal. I'm so sorry.

Wavey's eyes blaze . . . and then Quoyle realizes his mistake:

QUOYLE *(cont'd)*
Wavey. I meant to say Wavey.

WAVEY
Oh good. I feel much better.

QUOYLE
I wonder, Wavey, if you were ever going to tell me, Wavey, about your fucked up marriage.

This catches Wavey off-guard—she's utterly stunned.

Quoyle slumps down to the floor, and passes out.

Wavey looks down at him, her eyes stinging with anger and confusion.

EXT. WAVEY'S HOUSE—MORNING

The sun peeking over the horizon.

INT. WAVEY'S HOUSE—SAME

QUOYLE *wakes up on the living room sofa with a monumental hangover.*

He sees WAVEY *in the kitchen, in her bathrobe, efficiently bustling around, preparing breakfast.*

Quoyle stumbles to his feet and makes his way into the kitchen.

QUOYLE

Hey. Listen . . .

WAVEY
(all business)
I'm scrambling eggs. You gonna be able to eat?

QUOYLE

No.

Wavey doesn't even look at him, just keeps preparing breakfast.

QUOYLE *(cont'd)*
Maybe I should leave.

She doesn't disagree. But he makes no move to go. After a moment:

WAVEY
You forget where the door is?

Quoyle unsteadily heads for the back door.

Wavey keeps preparing breakfast, holding onto her shakey composure.

Quoyle opens the back door and leaves . . .

. . . and then Wavey's composure snaps: she impulsively THROWS THE FRYING PAN AGAINST THE WALL, *and half-cooked eggs splatter.*

EXT. OUTSIDE THE DOOR—SAME

QUOYLE *stands there. Wavey steps out into the cold wearing only her bathrobe, her face flush with rage.*

He ran off to Winnipeg with some little bitch barely out of high school. Is *that* fucked up enough for you?

Quoyle looks at her in confusion.

WAVEY *(cont'd)*

Herold. My husband. He didn't die. Not that he didn't deserve to.

Quoyle is bewildered: Herold didn't die?

WAVEY *(cont'd)*

He left me when I was eight months pregnant, and no good to him in bed.

Wavey gives Quoyle an acrid wink: here comes the good part:

WAVEY *(cont'd)*

So I took his fifteen-footer out into the Bay, cracked the hull with a hatchet, and sunk 'er. And pretended he was drowned. And played the grieving widow. And packed my bags to leave town.

Quoyle is trying to absorb what she's telling him.

WAVEY *(cont'd)*

But a funny thing happened. All these pathetic little folks I grew up with? They put their hearts around me and Herry. So we wouldn't be alone.
(*a* BEAT)
And I just couldn't leave.

She stares, bitterly, into Quoyle's eyes.

QUOYLE
(ashamed)

I'm sorry.

WAVEY

You're always sorry.

She goes back inside and shuts the door in his face.

INT. WAVEY'S HOUSE—SAME

WAVEY *stands there looking at the closed door. She wants to open it again—but doesn't.*

She turns and sees HERRY *in the hallway, in his pajamas, sleepily looking up at her.*

He takes her hand: an innocent, unselfconscious gesture.

And that simple little gesture is too much for Wavey: her eyes well up with tears. She pulls Herry to her and hugs him very tightly.

EXT. NUTBEEM'S TRAILER—MORNING

As QUOYLE *miserably shuffles up, we see that Nutbeem's trailer, like his boat, has been turned on its side and demolished; walls crushed and splintered. Sitting on the cinder blocks that once supported the trailer, Nutbeem, Billy, and Dennis swig beers.*

NUTBEEM
(amiably)
You're looking dishy, Quoyle.

Quoyle has never felt worse. Nutbeem hands him a beer.

NUTBEEM *(cont'd)*
I'm afraid my offer to let you stay in my trailer . . .
(indicates destroyed trailer)
. . . will have to be retracted.

QUOYLE
(deeply ashamed)
Sorry about that. And your boat.

BILLY

I'm some disgusted with the human race.

NUTBEEM

I never would've made it anyway. Storms would've blown
me to bits. You boys saved my life, I imagine.

The boys look at each other, humiliated by his generosity.

NUTBEEM *(cont'd)*

I've gathered my savings, and am flying back to Brazil.
Where the water is swimming pool green.

As a few flakes of SNOW *begin to fall, Nutbeem's choice seems
entirely logical.*

DENNIS
(to Quoyle)

You and Bunny can stay with the wife and me. Beety loves
kids.

QUOYLE

I wouldn't wanna impose—

DENNIS

Shut up and drink your beer.

BILLY
(a toast; without energy:)

To Brazil.

DENNIS/QUOYLE/NUTBEEM
(clinking beer bottles; without energy:)

To Brazil.

INT. KILLICK-CLAW GENERAL STORE—DAY

QUOYLE *and* BUNNY *(who's wearing a necklace made of Fruit
Loops cereal and string) enter the store—*

—and encounter WAVEY *and* HERRY *on their way out, almost literally bumping into them.*

BUNNY

Hi!

Herry and Bunny execute a clumsy high-five.

Quoyle looks profoundly uncomfortable in Wavey's presence.

WAVEY
(kneels down beside Bunny)
Love your necklace, Bunny. Can I feel it?

BUNNY
(proudly)
I used Fruit Loops, like you said.

QUOYLE
(awkwardly)
Hi, Wavey.

WAVEY
(polite, barely glancing at Quoyle)
Hello.
(to Bunny)
It's a very smart necklace. I love the way you used the colors.

BUNNY

Thanks.

WAVEY

(gives Bunny's hair a stroke)
See ya later, okay kiddo?

BUNNY

'kay.

Wavey rises, and leads Herry out of the store.

Quoyle stands there, watching Wavey walk away.

BUNNY *(cont'd)*

Aren't we gonna buy anything, Daddy?

QUOYLE

Hm? Oh.

Quoyle allows Bunny to lead him further into the store.

EXT. THE GREEN HOUSE—NIGHT

The wind is blowing, pale clouds scudding swiftly past the moon. The CABLES *of the Green House are* MOANING *their* HARSH SONG.

BUNNY *stands in the wind, with a parka over her pajamas, looking down at the crevice where the shrouded* DEAD BIRD *lies. Just silently staring at it.*

INT. THE GREEN HOUSE—SAME

QUOYLE *is asleep. Bunny enters, takes off her parka and slips into bed.*

CAMERA PUSHES IN *on* QUOYLE'S CLOSED, SLIGHTLY TWITCHING EYELIDS, *and . . .*

EXT. OCEAN—TWILIGHT

QUOYLE *is* UNDERWATER, *bubbles streaming from his mouth and nose. He thrashes and struggles toward the surface—but* BUMPS HIS HEAD *on a* SHEET OF ICE, *and realizes the surface is completely frozen.*

Quoyle spots a HOLE *in the ice, and clumsily struggles toward it. But just as he* SURFACES *through the hole, he sees:*

THE GREEN HOUSE *moving across the ice toward him, being pulled by the* ANCIENT QUOYLES—*along with* PETAL, *and* GUY QUOYLE AT AGE *15, and* AGNIS *at age 12. The* MOANING OF THE CABLES *is distorted and grotesque.*

The Green House moves heavily across the ice—right over the hole in the surface, FORCING QUOYLE BACK UNDER THE WATER. *He is thrashing helplessly underwater. Drowning.*

INT. THE GREEN HOUSE—KITCHEN—LATER (EARLY MORNING)

QUOYLE *sits alone at the kitchen table, once again with a cup of tea. He drinks it very slowly, lost in his unhappy thoughts. Then his eye wanders to:* THE BOOK OF ROBERT BURNS POETRY *tucked away on a high shelf.*

He goes over, takes the book.

> AGNIS (O.S.)
> Does that belong to you?

Quoyle sees Agnis entering the kitchen. A BEAT.

> QUOYLE
> There's still hot water in the kettle. Want some tea?

Agnis says nothing. Then she sits down at the table.

> QUOYLE *(cont'd)*
> *(fixing her a cup of tea)*
> Dennis says they've got room for me and Bunny.
> *(a BEAT)*
> You sure you'll be okay, over your shop?

> AGNIS
> I said I would, didn't I.

Quoyle stirs some sugar into Agnis's tea.

QUOYLE

I think you were right about Silver Melville cutting off her husband's head.

Agnis looks up at him: huh?

Quoyle sets down Agnis's tea in front of her.

QUOYLE *(cont'd)*

He probably deserved it. Maybe more women should do what she did.

Agnis looks at him dubiously.

QUOYLE *(cont'd)*
(softly)
Some women shoulda done it to their brother. My father.

Quoyle sits down across from her. She's staring at him.

QUOYLE *(cont'd)*

Cousin Nolan dropped by the other night.

Agnis keeps staring . . . sickened that Quoyle knows her secret.

She wants to deny it . . . but knows she can't.

Then Agnis stoically gets up and starts straightening up the kitchen, putting dishes into the cupboard.

But then she has to stop, because she can't see what she's doing—because, to her anger, she is crying.

She just stands there now. Quoyle goes to her, taking out his handkerchief—but she waves it away. Then she grabs the damn thing and blows her nose into it and lets the tears flow.

AGNIS

You know, I always thought if anyone knew about it, I'd be turned to stone.

She cries again into her handkerchief and laughs a bit, too. Quoyle puts an arm around her . . . and she stiffly allows herself to put an arm around him and pat him a few times.

>   AGNIS *(cont'd)*
> Shit.

She slumps down into her seat at the table. Quoyle sits down across from her.

>   QUOYLE
> Tea's a good drink. It'll keep you going.

She nods. They both sip their tea. Agnis wipes at her eyes, and re-composes herself.

>   QUOYLE *(cont'd)*
> When someone hurts you that much . . . how do you . . . ?
>   *(quietly; mostly to himself)*
> Does it ever go away? Is it possible . . . ?

His voice trails off.

Agnis studies him a moment. Then:

>   AGNIS
> Let me see the book.

Quoyle slides the ROBERT BURNS BOOK *over to Agnis.*

She opens it to a particular page. There's a PHOTO *tucked into the book.*

She takes out the photo, touches it lovingly. And now Quoyle sees it:

THE PHOTO *shows* AGNIS *(10* YEARS YOUNGER*) dancing with a* HANDSOME 50-ISH WOMAN *(IRENE)—cheek-to-cheek, very much in love.*

Quoyle is surprised, but says nothing.

> AGNIS *(cont'd)*
> Her name was Irene.

Agnis waits for Quoyle's reaction. He just gazes silently at the photo. Finally:

> QUOYLE
> *(re: picture)*
> You look happy.

Agnis takes a sip of tea. Quoyle does too.

> AGNIS
> So, yes. It is possible.

EXT. DENNIS AND BEETY'S HOUSE—AFTERNOON

DENNIS and his perky, aproned wife BEETY greet QUOYLE (who holds a suitcase) and BUNNY at the front door.

> DENNIS
> Welcome, weary travelers. Come in!

> BEETY
> Our home is your home.

> BUNNY
> *(a simple statement of fact)*
> No it's not.

> QUOYLE
> *(scolding)*
> Bunny . . .

> BEETY
> Come on in, sweetie—I made a big seal-flipper pie.

Beety puts a gentle hand on Bunny's shoulder, but Bunny silently turns away . . .

. . . and SEES *something in the sky:* A BALL OF WHITE LIGHT ROLLING ALONG THE HORIZON.

> BUNNY
>
> What's that?

They all watch it.

> BEETY
>
> Weather light. Storm comin'.

> DENNIS
>
> Big one.

EXT. OCEAN—DUSK

There's an IMPOSSIBLY HUGE BANK OF OMINOUS CLOUDS *massing along the horizon—suddenly illuminated by a gigantic flash of* LIGHTNING *that momentarily turns night into day.*

INT. A 12-PASSENGER COMMERICIAL AIRPLANE—DUSK

flying over the ocean. NUTBEEM, *wearing an absurdly festive Hawaiian shirt, gazes out the window at the massive storm gathering. He looks a little nostalgic . . . he's actually gonna miss this damn place.*

EXT. BILLY PRETTY'S HOUSE—DUSK

BILLY, *steeling himself against the winds of the gathering* STORM, *painstakingly resecures his boat's tether line to the dock.*

INT. ROOM ABOVE AGNIS'S SHOP—SAME

AGNIS, *in her nightgown, is sitting up in bed, calmly knitting, despite the furious sounds of the* STORM *outside.*

And lying beside Agnis in bed is: MAVIS BANGS, *also in a nightgown, contentedly reading* One Hundred Famous Mountie Stories.

Agnis and Mavis are the picture of domestic serenity, ignoring the raging storm.

INT. NOLAN QUOYLE'S HUT—DUSK

NOLAN'S BONY OLD HANDS *telling a length of knotted twine as if it were the rosary.*

> NOLAN
> *(whispers to the twine)*
> The house . . . The house . . .

Nolan's lips part in a brown-toothed smile. As he caresses the knotted twine, he is almost trembling with pleasure at what is conjuring.

INT. A BEDROOM IN DENNIS AND BEETY'S HOUSE—NIGHT

BUNNY *and* QUOYLE *are asleep in twin beds.* CAMERA PUSHES IN *on* QUOYLE'S ASHEN FACE, *which is briefly illuminated by* LIGHTNING . . .

QUOYLE'S DREAM:

He's SINKING UNDERWATER *once again. The water is* SPORADICALLY ILLUMINATED BY LIGHTNING *from a storm above.*

And now PETAL, *her eyes tranquil and benevolent, swims through the water to Quoyle and embraces him,* KISSES HIM *deeply,* PULLING HIM FARTHER AND FARTHER DOWN *through the the murky, lightning-lit water . . . and Quoyle, helpless with bliss, returns her fatal kiss—*

—*until with sudden anger Quoyle* BREAKS AWAY FROM PETAL'S EMBRACE *and* SWIMS FRANTICALLY TOWARD THE SURFACE—

—*and* PETAL GRABS FOR HIM, *and he flails and struggles to break free of her*—

—*and he kicks her away, and* BREAKS THROUGH THE SURFACE OF THE WATER, *and:*

ON THE WATER'S SURFACE

as Quoyle breaks through, GASPING FOR AIR, *and:*

QUOYLE WAKES UP FROM HIS DREAM

desperately GASPING FOR AIR. *Bunny stirs, but doesn't wake up.*

Quoyle recovers his breath . . . but he's still profoundly agitated, as if he has received a shattering revelation.

Impulsively Quoyle gets out of bed and grabs his clothes from a heap on the floor, and we:

CUT TO:

QUOYLE DRIVING HIS STATION WAGON

through the raging storm. The car is REPEATEDLY SKIDDING *on the snowy street, and is* BUFFETED BY THE DRIVING WIND.

THE CAR

SKIDS DANGEROUSLY *across the snowy road, and:*

QUOYLE STRUGGLES DESPERATELY WITH THE STEERING WHEEL, *somehow managing to keep the car on the road. He keeps right on driving, with steely resolve.*

INT. WAVEY'S HOUSE—NIGHT

HERRY *lies asleep.* WAVEY, *sitting in his bed, now puts aside a book of nursery rhymes that she obviously was reading to him earlier. She stands up and ties her bathrobe tighter against the chill air.* A TREE BRANCH, *buffeted by the fierce wind, is* BANGING *insistently against the window. Wavey goes to the window, gazing at the horrific storm outside.*

And then something down in the street catches her eye: QUOYLE'S STATION WAGON, *pulling up in front of the house. Wavey is amazed . . . and apprehensive.*

EXT. WAVEY'S YARD—NIGHT

QUOYLE *struggles to walk against the driving gale. He tramps past the play toys in the yard, which clatter nightmarishly in the wind.*

He reaches the front door. He's about to ring the bell . . . but hesitates. What could he possibly say to her?

Then the DOOR OPENS. *It's* WAVEY, *wordlessly looking at him.*

Quoyle steps inside.

INT. WAVEY'S HOUSE—HALLWAY—SAME

WAVEY *closes the door against the wind.*

She and QUOYLE *stand there looking at each other. Wavey looks at him coolly, warily, waiting for an explanation.*

Quoyle doesn't know where to begin. The door is BANGING *against the wall in the wind.*

> QUOYLE
> *(struggling to silence the door)*
> Wavey. I'm sorry—

WAVEY

Yeah, we covered that already. It's late, Quoyle, and it's cold. Do you have anything to say that I don't already know?

Quoyle considers this. He nods yes.

Without even a trace of ambivalence, he kissses her on the lips. She hesitates . . . and then kisses him back.

INT. WAVEY'S BEDROOM—MOMENTS LATER

Outside, the STORM IS RAGING EVEN MORE FIERCELY, *as* WAVEY *leads* QUOYLE *to the bed. They lie down together, kissing each other with increasing urgency, and he pulls the robe away from her body . . .*

INT. BEDROOM IN DENNIS AND BEETY'S HOUSE—NIGHT

BUNNY *asleep, alone. Suddenly her* EYES OPEN.

She gets out of bed and runs through the house in the dark, as the WIND SCREAMS ITS STRANGE WARNING.

Bunny races into the parlor, still looking wildly around—and the WIND SUDDENLY INVADES THE HOUSE *and begins to* BLOW BUNNY TOWARD THE DOOR—

—and the DOOR *is* THROWN OPEN *by the wind—and in a matter of seconds, the powerful wind* PULLS BUNNY RIGHT OUT THE DOOR, *and:*

CUT TO:

EXT. QUOYLE'S POINT—NIGHT

where BUNNY *has been* PINNED *against* A GRANITE BOULDER *by the force of the wind, just in front of the* GREEN HOUSE—*its* STEEL CABLES STRAINING AND SHRIEKING *against the wind.* A SHINGLE LIFTS, *torn off by the wind.*

BUNNY, *powerless to move, stares up at:*

A course of BRICKS FLYING OFF THE CHIMNEY *like playing cards. The* CABLES WAIL HORRIBLY.

EXT. THE GREEN HOUSE—SAME

BUNNY *watches as a cable* SNAPS. *Windows* BURST *like flashbulbs. The house slews. The snapped cable* WHIPS *wildly in the wind.*

And another cable SNAPS, *and then another . . . and the* HOUSE SLIDES FREE *along the rocks, toward the cliff, Bunny watching as the house goes over the edge and* TUMBLES *down toward the sea . . .*

INT. BEDROOM IN DENNIS AND BEETY'S HOUSE—DAWN

BUNNY *wakes up from her dream.*

QUOYLE *(still wearing his coat, having returned from Wavey's house) is entering the room. She looks up at him.*

> BUNNY
>
> It's gone.

> QUOYLE
>
> What?

> BUNNY
>
> The green house. I didn't dream it. Don't say I did.

Quoyle stares at her. Bunny rolls over to go back to sleep.

INT. DENNIS AND BEETY'S KITCHEN—MORNING

BEETY *has served a lovely looking breakfast for* QUOYLE, BUNNY, *and* DENNIS—*but Bunny, still shaken by her dream, doesn't touch her food.*

BEETY
(to Bunny)
Would you like some jam on your—

BUNNY
No.

Quoyle gives Beety an apologetic look. The PHONE RINGS.

DENNIS
(into phone)
Yeah. Well hi, Mumma—this is a surprise.

As Dennis listens, his face turns grave.

DENNIS *(cont'd)*
(into phone)
Oh. Oh my God . . .
(listens; then, near tears:)
Yeah. Of course.

He listens for another BEAT, *then somberly hangs up the phone. Beety looks at him worriedly.*

DENNIS *(cont'd)*
It's about my dad . . .

He's upset, unable to say another word.

EXT. UNDERWATER—OCEANBREAK—DAY

JACK BUGGIT'S BODY *is bobbing silently in the water. Above him, on the water's surface, is his overturned skiff (the "Maid in the Meadow").*

EXT. JACK BUGGIT'S HOUSE—DAY

People dressed in their Sunday best are arriving for Jack's wake.
QUOYLE, WAVEY, HERRY, BUNNY, AGNIS, *and* MAVIS *get out of Quoyle's station wagon.*

BUNNY
(explaining to Herry)
Mr. Buggit is sleeping with the angels.

Quoyle and Wavey exchange a sad glance.

BUNNY (cont'd)
But maybe he'll wake up.

QUOYLE
Bunny. He can't wake up. I *told* you—

BUNNY
Then why do they call it a "wake"?

This flummoxes Quoyle: good question.

INT. JACK BUGGIT'S HOUSE—MOMENTS LATER

The house is filled with people. There is eating and chatter; some
people trying to be cheerful, others just dazed with grief. QUOYLE
makes his way through the crowd to:

INT. THE KITCHEN—SAME

QUOYLE *finds* DENNIS *rummaging through kitchen drawers:*

DENNIS
Looking for Dad's lodge pin—

QUOYLE
Here. It was down at the office.

Quoyle holds out the LODGE PIN to dry-eyed EDNA BUGGIT,
who is being comforted by a weeping BEETY.

EDNA
(to Quoyle)
Would you write something for the *Gammy Bird*, about
Jack?

                              QUOYLE
                        (surprised, touched)
        I'll try.

INT. A BEDROOM—SAME

BUNNY, *stock-still, stares closely at* JACK'S BODY *lying on the bed, his face waxy and ashen. He is covered with a crocheted blanket, hands folded on his chest, eyes closed. A small cluster of people, including* BILLY, *stand by the bed in the darkened room.*

Billy, glass in hand, his face bloodred with whiskey, delivers a sort of improvised eulogy:

                              BILLY
        You all know we are only passing by. We only walk over
        these stones a few times.

Bunny is fascinated as she studies Jack. She sees a SLIGHT TREMOR *pass across Jack's face. She keeps watching intently.*

                        BILLY *(cont'd)*
        Our boats ride the waves a little while and then they have to
        sink.

EDNA, DENNIS, *and weeping* BEETY *enter, followed by* QUOYLE *and* WAVEY.

Quoyle goes to Bunny, and gently draws her away from her scrutiny of Jack's ashen face.

Edna leans with trembling hands to fix the Lodge Pin to Jack's lapel. Shaking, her hand lurches, the big pin goes PLUNGING, *and:*

A SOUND LIKE AN OLD ENGINE STARTING UP COMES OUT OF JACK'S CHEST, *then his head jerks on the pillow, salt water spills from his mouth, and his* EYES OPEN—*and everyone in the room is utterly bewildered. A miracle.*

DENNIS

Dad!

Dennis lunges to help his gurgling father free his shoulders from the coffin's wedge. Jack WHISPERS SOMETHING *in Dennis's ear. People are* SCREAMING, LAUGHING, CRYING—*every kind of reaction you could imagine. And in the midst of this complete bedlam, Bunny coolly tugs on Quoyle's sleeve:*

BUNNY

See? I told you.

CUT TO:

INT. THE DEN—A LITTLE LATER

DENNIS *is sorting through a stack of* DOCUMENTS. QUOYLE *and* BILLY *approach* . . .

DENNIS

It's gotta be in here somewhere!

QUOYLE

What—?

DENNIS

Dad's fishing license. That's what he whispered to me! He's gonna sign it over, seein' how he's beat the curse.

Quoyle and Billy exchange an intrigued glance.

Now they see, out in the hallway, PARAMEDICS *taking* JACK *out on a stretcher.*

BILLY

Holy Jesus, look at 'im—trying to sit up, and them poor paramedics tryin' to hold 'im down.

161

QUOYLE
(*realizing the irony:*)
Not very good at being sick, is he.

CUT TO:

EXT. IN FRONT OF JACK BUGGIT'S HOUSE—DAY

Everyone watches JACK, *on a stretcher, being carried out of the house by the* PARAMEDICS.

BUNNY *is standing between* QUOYLE *and* WAVEY.

BUNNY
Can we have a wake for Petal?

Quoyle and Wavey exchange an uneasy glance.

BUNNY (*cont'd*)
(*indicating Jack*)
Well it worked for him.

WAVEY
Bunny. They thought he was dead, but it was a mistake. It was more like he was in a coma.

The Paramedics bang Jack's stretcher against the ambulance as they load him in:

JACK
(*weak but feisty*)
Don't bang it so!

PARAMEDIC
It's best if you don't talk—

JACK
If the damn ocean couldn't shut me up, whadaya think your chances is?

BUNNY
(to Wavey and Quoyle)
Maybe Petal's in one of those. A coma.

QUOYLE
Bunny . . . Petal's never coming back.

Bunny considers this.

BUNNY
(to Wavey)
Is that true?

WAVEY
Yes. It's true.

Quoyle steels himself to tell it straight:

QUOYLE
Petal is dead, Bunny. Like that bird you found, with the
broken neck.

Wavey intently watches Quoyle as he talks to Bunny:

QUOYLE *(cont'd)*
I'm sorry. I shouldn't have said Petal's asleep.

Bunny absorbs it . . . and nods, without comment. Okay.

Now Billy comes up to Quoyle:

BILLY
Listen, Quoyle, in all the confusion I never did get a chance
to tell you . . . how awful sorry I was to hear about your
house.

Quoyle gives Billy a puzzled look.

BILLY *(cont'd)*
(a BEAT*; surprised:)*
You mean nobody's told you?

EXT. QUOYLE'S POINT—DAY

QUOYLE, WAVEY, BUNNY, HERRY, AGNIS AND MAVIS
*emerge from Quoyle's station wagon, and all of them are astonished
to see that* THE GREEN HOUSE IS GONE—*all of them, that is,
except for Bunny.*

> BUNNY
> *(calmly to Quoyle)*
See? I told you.

Quoyle gapes at the bare expanse of rock.

> QUOYLE
> *(trying to comfort her)*
Aunt . . .

> AGNIS
Oh, it's alright. Worse things have happened. To both of us.

They survey the scene in silence. Then:

> AGNIS *(cont'd)*
Maybe someday we'll build a little summer place out here.

Quoyle thinks about it. What a concept:

> QUOYLE
Summer.

> BUNNY
> *(earnestly)*
Do they have summer up here?

                    AGNIS
                  (to Bunny)
You'll know it's summer when the partridge-berries come
out.

                    WAVEY
                  (to Bunny)
And you can make partridge-berry duff, and sweet
berryocki.

Bunny eyes Wavey for a long moment.

                    BUNNY
Will you teach me how?

                    WAVEY
                (a BEAT; touched:)
Yeah. I will. Yeah.

Now Bunny notices something nearby:

                    BUNNY
Hey—it flew away!

She's looking at the little CREVICE *in the rocks where she interred
the dead bird.*

                  BUNNY *(cont'd)*
Daddy, the bird—it flew away.

Quoyle takes a closer look: the BIRD IS GONE—*but the*
KLEENEX *is* STILL THERE, *stuck in between the rocks exactly
where Bunny once placed it.*

*Quoyle doesn't know quite how to answer. He looks at Agnis, whose
wise eyes seem to say: don't even try.*

*Wavey takes Quoyle's hand. Bunny reaches out and takes Wavey's
other hand . . . and Herry, following suit, snuggles up against
Quoyle . . .*

. . . and then: Agnis calmly slips her arm around Mavis's waist. It's unmistakable: the casually affectionate gesture of a lover. Quoyle sees this, but says nothing; he just gives Agnis an approving nod.

Then the six of them gaze out at the ocean in calm silence.

Looking out at the sparkling water, they are comfortable and serene in each other's company.

Just like a family.

FADE OUT.